PRINCESS ROURAN

& the Dragon Chariot of 10,000 Sages

Shawe Ruckus

Chapter 1

A roar.

Profound and prolonged.

Moli imagined a dragon soaring in the sky.

Not a medieval beast that torched villages and harmed lives, but a Chinese dragon.

Yes, a dragon.

Its body stretching for miles, its golden scales gleaming, its gossamer whiskers floating in mid-air, its claws strong. A dragon that directs wind and rain, a dragon that sends lightning and thunder.

Of course, Moli had never seen a dragon, but she had interacted with one many times in her imagination.

A few months earlier, Moli's fascination with dragons had become a topic of conversation in her house. Her grandfather had teased her from time to time with the story of Lord Ye, who loved dragons.

Lord Ye was a man from an ancient era in China who was obsessed with dragons. He had collected many dragon-themed artefacts and even carved dragons on the pillars in his house. One day, a dragon who had heard about Lord Ye's fascination decided to pay a friendly visit. As soon as the dragon appeared, Lord Ye escaped in shock, yelling for help.

Moli had told her grandpa that she would never run away if she saw a real dragon. She wondered if dragons could speak human languages.

On her birthday, her uncle had gifted her a complete illustrated edition of *The Classic of Mountains and Seas*. She was awestruck at the many mythical creatures and natural wonders as she flipped through the pages. She was so absorbed with her reading that she wore her slippers the wrong way.

Another roar.

Moli closed her eyes, not daring to move.

She had heard that a dragon's roar was like a cow's moo.

Rumour had it that Moli's great-grandmother had seen a real dragon. More than once, Moli had pestered her grandma to tell her the story of the dragon, and her grandma always began like this:

"It was the summer of 1934. My mother was only seven or eight years old. A fellow villager said a dragon had fallen to Yingkou and needed their help. The whole village went to rescue the dragon. Some carried jars of water, some took gourds, and some took straw mats. When they got there, they poured water onto the dragon and used the mats to keep its skin moist. You know, many said that saving a dragon was a remarkable feat that could bring fortune to people for several lifetimes. The villagers had also invited Buddhist monks to chant mantras. It rained so heavily that the river swelled. Then, one day, the dragon soared up into a storm and disappeared. Sometime later, I couldn't say if it was a month or a week, the villagers heard that the dragon had crashed. Some elders cried because that was a bad omen."

Every time Moli heard this story, she recalled the 'whale fall' she had once seen in a documentary – when a whale dies in the ocean, its body gradually sinks to the ocean floor and provides nourishment for other sea creatures along the way.

If there is a whale fall, could there be a 'dragon fall'?

Do dragons die?

She had searched many times online for information about the 'dragon fall incident'. Some said that the 'dragon' was a stranded whale; some said it was a scheme invented by the invading Japanese army to cause panic, and some said...

Someone was talking.

The phrases 'closed-loop', 'ecosystem', and 'dimensionality reduction' drifted into her ears. Moli opened her eyes and adjusted her mask, her breath cooling on the tip of her nose. She rose and looked back. Two rows of seats away, several adults with masks and face shields were conversing.

The aisles of the flight cabin were cold and empty.

In between the roar of the plane's engines, Moli could vaguely hear the words 'KPI' and 'growth forecast'. Someone had also said 'tofu'.

Perhaps someone was hungry...

Moli checked the remaining flight time on the seat screen. Five more hours to go...

"Moli. Don't cry. You are a strong girl."

She remembered her grandmother's words.

Someone explained the meaning of 'tofu'; it meant the 'top of the funnel'.

What a funny phrase. Moli looked over at her mother in the next seat, sleeping soundly, her fingers curled around the edge of her jacket.

Moli had been interested in words and languages before she became fascinated with dragons. Whenever she heard or saw a word, whether it was in Mandarin or English, she tried to paint a scene in her mind.

Once in class, her English teacher, Miss Warner, was explaining the word 'bank'.

Moli raised her hand and told the class to imagine the word. 'B' is a pebbled riverbank, 'a' the handrails on the bridge; 'n' was an arch of a bridge, and 'k' is an estuary where birds tread water catching small fish.

Miss Warner interrupted her and said that was not necessary. The class only needed to remember 'bank' as a financial institution and not a river feature.

Moli retorted, "Textbooks cannot include everything that matters in life! If someone went to the South Bank in London and saw the words, would they think they were in a big bank?"

After class, Miss Warner summoned Moli and asked her why she had embarrassed her in front of the whole class. Moli was unhappy for a long time.

However, she soon had a chance to get even with her teacher.

In their after-school activity a week later, the class had played Scrabble with Miss Warner. And at the end, Moli spelt the word 'anus' and gained enough points to win. Before anyone else could ask what the word meant, Miss Warner dismissed the class, saying their session was over.

Recalling that afternoon, Moli snickered in her seat.

The plane had met turbulence, and the seatbelt indicator lit up. Moli resettled into her seat. Her movements might have woken her mother.

"Maggie, I've just learned a new word called 'tofu'. Do you want to know what it means?" Moli asked as she buckled her seat belt.

"Get some more sleep."

Moli pretended to close her eyes.

The small group meeting down the aisle was over, and the only sounds left in the cabin were the mechanical notes and the footsteps of the flight attendants returning to their seats.

Before Maggie had become Moli's mom, she had run into Morris while studying on a postgraduate course in London. Their encounter was somewhat clichéd and began with a mix-up of their umbrellas. Then a union and a separation.

While Morris worked as a historian touring Central Asia, Maggie and Moli had returned to China. Then Maggie had met 'strategy' at work.

Moli first learned about 'strategy' from a picture book. It meant 'plan of attack'. She had once taken notes that, in one month, her mother had said the words 'strategy' and 'product innovation' at home more than she had called Moli's name. But as bad as 'strategy' was, Maggie had stayed, while Morris kept himself busy researching history.

Moli didn't like history.

She didn't like memorising chronologies, dates, and names of historical figures.

When the COVID-19 pandemic started, the adults always said that they were witnessing history.

She didn't want to witness such history.

Moli remembered an older girl she had met at the 'Big Whale' last summer. The Big Whale was a metal artwork near Moli's neighbourhood, right on the shoreline. It depicted a mother whale with her child and reached up to three storeys tall.

The first time Moli met the girl on the beach, she had also taught Moli a new phrase in English – 'longshore drift', which means the process of how sand drifts along the coast. Moli tried to picture this word. A grain of sand, longing for the shore, only to drift far away with the waves.

The summer ended, and the Big Whale sister left to study in the US and was never heard from again.

"Umm..." Moli heard Maggie sighing.

Some time ago, one of the foreign teachers at Moli's school had sent a group email to all the parents and students. Her mother sighed after reading it.

The subject line of the email was: YOU SHOULD APOLOGISE FOR THE VIRUS!

Before Moli could read any further, Maggie had logged onto Zoom and sent her away.

The school staff and parents had gone to great lengths not to let the children see the email, but still, someone took a screenshot and spread it in their secret chat groups. After reading the email, Moli felt for the first time that words can hurt people deeply.

Moli's uncle, a clinical neuroscientist, told her: "Moli, we don't need to apologise, but we must say thank you. We need to thank everyone who cared for everyone else's lives and health. A big thank you to all the medical staff, the workers who built the emergency hospitals, the volunteers who delivered food and essential supplies during the lockdowns, compatriots overseas who raised money, and foreign governments who donated masks and goods. When we were in great need, many people lent a helping hand, and we will do our best to help them. Yes, we had first reported the virus in Wuhan. *Post hoc, ergo propter hoc.* Spanish flu did not originate in Spain. Japanese encephalitis was only so named because it was first reported by a Japanese doctor. Now, increasing evidence has suggested that the virus had quietly spread in other countries before we identified it. We have found many cases where the virus stayed on the packaging of frozen food items. Could it be that the virus came to Wuhan through cold chain logistics? Conclusions should only come after global investigations, and not before." Her uncle paused. "Is it not the case that the Chinese character for 'human' is two strokes supporting each other? This is not the time to point fingers at each other; this is the time for us to hold hands."

Time to hold hands. Moli remembered one time when she was still small. Her parents took her for a walk in Hyde Park.

They held her hands, Maggie on the left and Morris on the right. They watched the swans and shared a vanilla ice cream in a cone.

When was the last time they had held hands?

She could not recall.

Now, on their way to Morris's funeral, Moli regretted deeply.

Now her dad had become a part of history.

Chapter 2

"Moli, would you like some tea downstairs?" Aunt Edith knocked and asked.

"No." Moli sat up in bed. Even after the quarantine, the time difference still made her dizzy.

"Are you sure? Not even some jasmine tea?" Edith came into the room. She looked preoccupied. "You must be exhausted."

"Some jasmine tea sounds nice." Moli straightened up and stretched. Through the window, she could see the residence across the street and a lady standing in the front porch, staring at her unwelcomingly.

"Oh, don't mind that old dragon. Here." Edith handed Moli her jumper and drew the curtains on the way.

Old dragon... Moli wondered why most of the English words about dragons were derogatory. An 'old dragon' is an annoying old person, and a 'dragon lady' is an evil female.

Were there any positive words using the word 'dragon'? She remembered the phrase 'dragon market', used to describe the burgeoning economies of Southeast Asia, and 'pendragon', a word that describes a leader in the British army in olden times.

Moli could almost see a dragon, holding a pen, wagging its tail, singing 'Pen-Pineapple-Apple-Pen'.

"Did you sleep well?" Edith smoothed a lock of Moli's hair for her.

"Yes." Moli put on her jumper and followed Edith downstairs. She could hear a cat meowing on the way down.

There were sour smells of old carpet and brewed coffee, and there were photo frames that garnished the wall above the wooden banister.

Photos of Morris and Edith.

One was of him with his family at the Great Wall; one was of him with the terracotta warriors; one was of a childhood birthday, with cream from the cake on his face; one was of his university graduation – he held his diploma in his arms, the word 'History' printed on the paper. The last was of him and Moli sitting on a small boat in a park, with a couple of swans and ducks stealing the show.

And there were pictures of Edith.

Pictures of her with her father and deceased mother, pictures of her fencing, pictures of her with Morris, pictures of her singing at her best friend's wedding.

Carved into the handrail of the staircase were the heights of the two children when they were young.

People say that every family has its problems, but every family should have its happy moments too. How many families have been robbed of their joy by the pandemic? Moli thought.

More cat meows. She followed the sound and found a ginger cat curled up in the corner of the room.

Intermittent talking came from the next room.

"He was away on a project and he travelled back..."

Moli's grandmother was talking to Maggie about Morris.

Moli tried to approach the cat, but it quickly sailed away.

"Don't worry," Edith explained, "he doesn't know you yet. He hasn't been close to anyone since his ma...disappeared."

Moli had guessed why and hoped she was wrong.

The conversation in the next room continued.

"I wanted Moli to come and study here. I know a very good girls' independent but I'm not so sure anymore," Moli heard her grandmother say.

"What's wrong, Moli?" Her aunt seemed to have sensed her uneasiness.

Edith did not understand Chinese.

"Nothing, Aunt Edith." Moli shook her head and followed Edith into the drawing room, which Moli always thought was an odd name, as no one had ever drawn in it.

"Ah, Moli. I've just made tea." Grandma Hua switched to English; she stood up and clasped Moli's hands. Grandma Hua was a third-generation Chinese in the UK. "Here's some nice jasmine tea to warm you up." Her grandmother lifted the white porcelain teapot and poured two cups of tea. Moli and Edith sat down around the table.

"Edith, how is your social project in London? Is it going well?" Maggie asked.

Edith's eyes lit up. "Well. We've had a hard time distributing the sanitary products to the homeless at the centralised shelters during the lockdown. Our original plan was to convert some of the old phone booths into temporary public toilets, but now it seems difficult."

They didn't talk about Morris anymore, perhaps out of concern for Moli. Her grandmother held onto the teapot tightly.

Moli raised her cup of tea, the aroma of jasmine soothing her. She stared at the glowing liquid in the cup, reflecting the light of the house.

Moli wondered what the colour of Meng Po's soup was. She wondered if Morris had already taken his share of the soup. Then he must have forgotten his family, his work, and even history.

They could never hold hands again.

Moli rushed to take a few sips from her cup, trying to blink back her tears.

"More tea?" Grandma asked with concern.

"No, thank you." Moli stood up. There was a pile of magazines on the settee. "Can I take a look?"

"Of course. The top one...page twenty-three has your father's last project, now on display at the British Museum."

Moli flipped through the bilingual magazine. Page twenty-three was titled 'The Lost Dynasty of Rouran'.

'If you have never heard of the Rouran dynasty, then you must have heard of Hua Mulan. Rouran was the enemy of Northern Wei, and Mulan joined the army for her father to resist the invasion of the Rourans.'

Moli remembered a cartoon she'd seen a long time ago. She liked that small dragon. She read on.

'The Rourans were the first to have used the words 'Khan' or 'Khagan'. The Rouran dynasty was active from the late fourth century to the middle of the sixth century CE. Their main nomadic range extended throughout what is now Mongolia, the Baikal region of Serbia and Russia, Central Asia, and China. The

Rourans believed in witchcraft and natural spirits, but hundreds of their people also converted to Buddhism. They had a strict military regime. This tour includes…'

"Say, I've just run into old Joey." There was a noise in the corridor.

They heard Edith's father grousing.

"He bought a truckload of bog rolls." Grandpa Orozco came into the room carrying two linen shopping bags. "Sorry, ladies, I've kept you all waiting. I will start dinner preparations now." He took off his mask and undid his scarf. "Now, Moli, what would you like for dessert?"

"Hmmm…" Moli hesitated, "I think some chocolate would be nice."

"Very well. I will make some brownies." Grandpa Orozco gave her a smile. "I might need an assistant. You know how to measure the ingredients and weigh the flour?"

"Sure." Moli closed the magazine and put it back.

Grandpa Orozco exchanged a glance with Moli's grandmother.

"Edith, why don't you join us? I know I've tried your patience, but I must ask you again for advice on what to do with that smart speaker; it always seems to disobey my commands. I want Premier League, it plays rock; I want the radio, it gives me poetry. Oh, I'm so worried. If I say *galleta*, it might as well buy me a *gallina*. To be honest, I still haven't found where its intelligence lies."

Before leaving the room, Moli heard Grandma and Maggie resume their conversation in Mandarin.

***

Later, after dinner, as Moli passed the drawing room, she saw the ginger cat lying on the settee, its front paws pressing against the magazine on Rouran.

"Don't be afraid," she told the cat as she approached the settee. "I just want to have a read."

Moli picked up the magazine and quickly retreated to the hallway.

Back in their room, Maggie had switched on the light and double-checked the windows. Then she took out an adapter and charged her laptop.

"Maggie..." Moli held the magazine, "I..."

Her mother gestured for her to sit down.

Moli found the article on Rouran again. "I was wondering if we could see this exhibition before we go back home?"

"Moli, I have a meeting at the London office tomorrow. I thought you might spend another day here with Grandma Hua and Edith?"

"Aunt Edith said she'd accompany me if you agreed. She's had the vaccines."

Maggie thought for a while. "All right then. But promise me you'll stay close to Edith. Don't run around, wear a mask all the time, remember to take your phone, don't touch any dogs or cats on the streets and watch out for mice."

"Oh, Maggie!" Moli voiced her discontent. "I'm not a three-year-old anymore."

Her mother looked at her sombrely and Moli decided to change the subject. "Maggie, do you know Rouran? Tell me about it."

"Let me see," Maggie smiled. "Truth be told, we are connected to the Rourans."

Moli took off her slippers and moved up the bed with her mother side by side.

"Really? How?" she wondered. "Isn't Rouran an ancient dynasty?"

"Did you know that we have a book on family records back home? It was about a clan of 'Ru' people from Yunzhong. They were descendants of the Rourans. Yunzhong is now known as 'Togtoh'. It's a county in Inner Mongolia."

"Even so, Grandpa was..." Moli paused.

Maggie's father had been orphaned by the Japanese invasion during World War Two. He was adopted and raised by a couple in Inner Mongolia.

"Moli, do you know that the famous writer Lu Xun said that 'under the boundless skies, amid a multitude of people, everyone concerns me'? As my Strategy professor once said, 'strategy' is about thinking where we were, how we got there, and where we want to go next. Perhaps now more than ever is the time for us to think about our history. Even something that you thought was so distant and far away concerns us. And it connects us still. Leonardo da Vinci said that everything connects to everything else, we simply don't know it yet."

"Connected," Moli murmured.

Maggie lowered her head and found her daughter asleep. She pulled the comforter over Moli, then got up and sat at the desk and opened her laptop.

There were faint sounds of rain and the distant sounds of bicycle brakes.

The house hadn't changed much since the last time she'd been there.

Except... Maggie picked up her phone, unlocked it, and found a message.

*Take care of Moli, and thank you for
being a part of my history.*

She pulled back her thoughts and decided to recheck tomorrow's presentation deck.

Chapter 3

The next day, Moli, Maggie, and Edith boarded the first train to London.

There were only a few passengers, and while Maggie busied herself with revising her presentation deck, Edith told Moli some interesting episodes about her time at university.

For example, her university's mascot was a lion, while the rival's was a penguin. And there was a mysterious bar in the university's Department of Philosophy. No one knows where it is precisely; if you wish to go there, you need to have a secret code and someone willing to guide you.

Maggie had completed her postgraduate studies at the same university that Edith attended, yet Moli had never heard these stories.

Edith also told her that there were the remains of a Roman baths inside a building on campus and an open-air ice rink next door. But the ice rink had been closed for some time.

They got off the train at Paddington. Maggie instructed Moli once again to stay close to her aunt and asked Edith one more time to keep a close eye on Moli, then she hurried to the Underground.

Moli looked around; there were only a few people on the platform, standing far apart. A few signs and posters reminded people about social distancing and the fine for not wearing a face covering.

"Looking for a bear?" Edith asked smilingly. "We should bring some marmalade; it might come in handy."

Moli made a face. "Aunt Edith, Peter Rabbit and Paddington are really cute, but I'm all grown up!"

"Children nowadays." Edith gestured Moli towards the exit. "I still remember, on my eleventh birthday, I was so eager and anxious to receive my acceptance letter from Hogwarts. I kept all the windows open late at night, every night, in case the owl messengers couldn't get in." She paused. "Morris was preparing for his A-Levels. He had Post-it notes in many places, with bits of historical knowledge, facts and figures on them. One day, the wind was so strong that all of his notes got mixed up. He didn't chide me. Then...I guess I had to accept that I probably wasn't going to become a witch."

"Aunt Edith, will you tell me more about my dad?"

"Hmm... let me think," Edith pondered. "He is..."

Past tenses now, she reminded herself.

"He...he was always a good student. He was a Prefect at his school. There was only one thing that ever-bothered Hua, and that was that Morris would bite his nails. She would check his nails three times a day. With a lot of effort, he finally stopped biting them."

Edith reflected as she led Moli to the bus stop. "Oh, and another time, my father heard Morris talking in his sleep, quite loudly. Morris was saying something about an 'odd van'. You see, my father volunteered for the Neighbourhood Watch, so he spent days looking out for any strangers who had vans and trucks. It turned out that there were no 'odd vans', but Morris meant 'Oldowan', a historical term used to describe the Palaeolithic culture of Africa. When I was still a child, and Hua would sometimes ask him to babysit me – he didn't call it babysitting, but 'an ethnographic study of a *Homo sapiens*' offspring'."

Moli had remained silent for a long time, and Edith noticed. "Moli, are you alright?"

"I...I'm thinking about beans."

"Beans? You mean...Mr Bean?" Edith was puzzled.

"No, no. I'm thinking about mung beans." Moli tilted her head. "Aunt Edith, if I tell you something, can I trust you not to tell the others?"

"A secret?" Edith thought for a while. "You can trust me to make a sound decision. But if it's something concerning your safety, then..."

"Let's make a pinkie promise first."

Edith did so gladly.

"Okay. Now I can tell you." Moli paused. "Once upon a time..."

"Hold on," Edith stopped her, joking, "the opening sounds a little familiar."

"Well, it was a long time ago. At least before the pandemic," Moli reminisced.

Their bus came, and they climbed up to the upstairs of the double-decker. A poster on the window said 'maximum capacity of 14 passengers'. Moli and Edith took separate seats and resumed their talk.

"Once..." Moli cleared her throat, "I went to a classmate's house for a sleepover. There were some other kids from our class. My classmate's grandfather looked after us, but he was tired, and he went to bed early. Then my classmate's older brother asked if we wanted to do something exciting, something *cool*."

"Moli, you see," Edith's expression grew serious, "whether it's a teacher, or a friend's family, or a neighbour, or a stranger, no matter the place, the time, the person, if you encounter any inappropriate physical or verbal actions, you will say it's wrong. You will stop it. You will tell the adults or the police. Don't be afraid. There's no need to be afraid."

"I know, Aunt Edith." Moli nodded vigorously. "I know. But what I'm about to say is a little different from what you think."

"Sorry." Edith motioned for her to continue.

"And then his brother showed us a Korean horror movie. Whenever the ghost appeared, there was a 'dong, dong, dong' sound, like a walking stick hitting the ground. And when the people in the movie heard the noise, they knew the ghost was coming for revenge."

Moli swallowed. "Of course, they'd all done bad things, so the ghost was after them." She stopped and looked at Edith. "The film was in Korean, and there were no subtitles. I only understood the pictures but not why the ghost was avenging. It was a scary movie. But that's not all..." Moli hesitated. "After a month or so, one time, in the middle of the night when I was sleeping, I started hearing the 'dong, dong, dong' sound. I was so scared. I hadn't done anything wrong. At least I hoped I hadn't, except...except for one time I won a Scrabble game not so...honestly. I tried to pretend that I was asleep, but the sound continued. I didn't dare to get out of the bed or open my eyes for fear that if I did, I would see the ghost right in front of my eyes or on the ceiling. I was sweating so much my hair was wet."

"Good grief! What happened next?" Edith asked nervously.

"The sound continued all night." Moli smiled sadly. "When it was early morning, I heard my grandpa going into the living room, and I jumped out of bed to look for him. He said that he'd heard a noise during the night that kept him awake. He thought that the tap in the kitchen might have been broken. We ventured into the kitchen..."

The bus stopped at a junction, and a couple of pigeons tap-danced on the crosswalk.

Moli laughed again, this time more boldly. "We found a bag of mung beans in the kitchen. The package had a leak, and so the beans had rolled down the chopping board to the sink, one by one, and every time a bean dropped into the sink, it made a 'dong' sound."

Edith sighed softly.

"And my grandma made a delicious mung bean pancake for lunch that day." Moli looked out of the window. "You know, Aunt Edith, sometimes I cannot quite figure myself out. After this incident, I concluded that there are no ghosts in the world. But... but sometimes I also believe that there are dragons and magic. And I wish that there were a Naihe Bridge and Meng Po's soup, and that people do reincarnate when they die."

"What bridge...and what soup?" Edith was perplexed.

Moli sniffed back a tear. "In Chinese folklore, when a person dies, they have to walk across the Naihe Bridge. After crossing it, an elderly lady, called Meng Po, will give the deceased a bowl of soup. When people drink the soup, they will forget that lifetime. Legend says that there are two ways that Meng Po makes her soup: one is by using people's souls and rare herbs; the other is to use her tears." Moli looked out of the window again. "After drinking the soup, people forget their past lives so they can be reborn in their next. Sometimes I wonder if my dad had already drunk the soup, but other times, I know that sounds unscientific."

The story had reminded Edith of Charon and Lethe from Greek mythology.

"It reminds of Lethe," she said, "a river in Greek mythology and when...departed souls drink its water, they forget their previous life on earth. How should I put it," she deliberated. "I think our thinking is like a library. There's a library inside the Warburg Institute – not far from the British Museum, actually. With most libraries, you have books categorised like this: first a broad theme, say history, then sub-divisions – European History, Asian History, Latin American history. Then you have more sub-divisions – the Scramble for Africa, World War Two. Then you have books arranged on the shelves by authors' information. But it's not like this in the Warburg Library. All books there are divided into four main categories and arranged on four floors: 'Action, Orientation, Word, and Image'. So, you'll find recipes next to books about magic, nursery rhymes next to books about war."

Edith thought for a while. "I think that sometimes our thinking is not unlike the Warburg Library. We summon the relevant contents – our cherished memories when we need courage – then we go to another floor when we need comfort, and another shelf when we need rationality."

Ding! A passenger put away his crossword puzzle and pushed the bell, startling Edith.

"This is us." Edith stood up and took Moli's hand. "Come on; we can talk on our way to the front gate."

They got off the bus from the rear door.

The air was cold and crisp, and the smell of cars' exhausts mixed with disinfectants wafted up Moli's nose. They walked down the street and waited for a light. Sleet began to fall.

Edith led the way. "I hope there won't be too many people today. Rumour has it that it'd take you a full two years and five months to go through the British Museum to read all the annotation tags. We can go and see the most famous pieces first. Like the Rosetta Stone, which helped historians to decipher Egyptian hieroglyphs. Then we'll go to the exhibition on Rouran."

Rouran...

Moli repeated this word in her head. It still sounded so distant.

"SHAME ON YOU!" a sharp voice shrilled, piercing the solemness in the air.

Edith was alarmed. She looked ahead to find that a commotion had gathered: a middle-aged woman was confronting two other people by the museum's entrance. An Asian man who held a long, furled, olive-green umbrella and a lady stood beside him.

"Do we know each other?" the Asian man asked.

"SHAME ON YOU! YOU SHAMELESS SLAG!" the woman shouted. "YOU TRAITOR! YOU WHOR–"

"Enough is enough. I won't allow you to insult my wife. Shame on me? You are the one condemning without cause. Shame on you." The man spoke with a charming lilt.

Edith stood beside Moli, and she hugged her tightly.

"Sir, I'm sorry to have offended you. My wife must have mistaken you as a...as a Chinese," another man apologised hurriedly.

"That's the only mistake she didn't make. I am Chinese. And I accept your apology if it's sincere, although it leaves much to be desired. I often consider apologies as futile if people's words don't align with their actions."

"YOU EAT EVERYTHING!" the woman shouted again, and suddenly Moli understood.

"I've never eaten a bat nor a pangolin, but I think I do know what an armadillo might taste like. According to your fellow countryman, Charles Darwin, it tastes like a duck. Maybe a lame duck. He particularly fancied puma, praising it as 'remarkably like veal in taste' and the contents of the bladder of a tortoise bitter. Perhaps allow me to remind you of some of your more refined culinary customs? Mummies as a popular side dish for many European families."

"YOU OWE US! YOU OWE US TOO BLOODY MUCH!"

"Your attire convinces me that you are from the 21st century, yet your repertoire of reasoning makes me wonder if you are not from the 19th century. I don't recall an occasion when I had borrowed anything or asked any favours from you," the man replied fluently, "but you did remind me to ask: do you suppose that the twenty-three thousand Chinese objects stored in the British Museum were all acquired legally and fairly?"

"YOU ARE ALL LIARS! THAT'S WHAT YOU ARE! LIARS!"

"If you insist, I have a story to tell, and it is called 'Two Bandits'."

"LIARS! SHAMELESS LIARS!"

"One day, two bandits entered the Summer Palace. One plundered, the other burned. Mixed up in all this is the name of Elgin, which inevitably calls to mind the Parthenon. What was done to the Parthenon was done to the Summer Palace, more thoroughly and better, so that nothing would be left. And back they came to Europe, *arm in arm*, laughing away. Such is the story of the two bandits. You Europeans are the civilised ones, and we Chinese are the barbarians. This is what civilisation has done to barbarism—"

"SHUT YOUR MOUTH!"

"Oh. These words were by Victor Hugo."

"YOU ARE ALL BRAINWASHED!"

"Are we?" The man smiled faintly. "Perhaps only the drunk ones don't say they are drunk. The worst is having a blotto *larghetto*."

Moli felt as though she was watching a play, except she was also a part of it. She wanted to stop the woman's shouting. Her dad would not have wanted to witness this, not here anyway...

A museum staff member rushed out, trying to maintain order.

The man enunciated, "When you've decided to let your mouth puke shit, that entitles people's *savoir-vivre* a hiatus." He thought for a while. "I sense that you are all weighed down by the white man's burden." Having said this, the man led his companion into the museum.

"Don't worry, Moli. It's all over. It's over," Edith whispered, not sure if she was comforting herself or Moli.

Moli looked at the bystanders again, feeling unsettled.

***

They took a moment to collect themselves and followed the black iron fence and found their way to the entrance. The Museum's colonnade resembled the colour of sheep that had rolled in mud all day long.

Moli followed Edith through the security check and used the hand sanitiser by the entrance. Once inside, the Museum looked like a giant butterfly ready to leap with its black grid-like ceiling, the white round reading room in the centre, and the two spiral staircases on the left and right.

As they passed the information counter, Moli overheard someone asking where the chair that Karl Marx sat in was.

Edith first showed Moli a large stone called the Rosetta Stone, then the Arabian bronze hand, and then the collection of marble sculptures called the Elgin Marbles from the temple of the Parthenon. Someone in the gallery was explaining that the Greek government was still urging the British government to return these marble artefacts to Athens.

Then they went up to the second floor and instated themselves in front of a mummified cat from Egypt. The cat had prominent eyes that reminded Moli of a Sphynx cat she had once seen on

TV. Edith thought of telling Moli about the *Book of the Dead*, then decided against it.

They wandered around for an hour while Edith enthusiastically told Moli the stories behind many objects and collections. Moli listened, but not attentively. She felt a little guilty. But all she heard was a bunch of names, places, dynasties, and more names.

Compared to the other rooms, the exhibit of Rouran was relatively compact and deserted, seemed that no one had valued Morris' last work.

Edith looked around. "Well. I have to admit, Moli, I don't know a lot about Rouran, so we'll learn together." She patted Moli lightly on the shoulder. "Take your time."

Moli nodded. She approached the first display case tentatively. There was a mask under rather dim light. It was made of gold foil; its design not so proportional. Two red jewels marked the eyes, and it had many small dots on the nose and either side of the cheeks that shaped into tree branches.

She checked the explanatory note: this was a female gold funerary mask from the Rouran period, unearthed in Kyrgyzstan in 1958. The tree branches resembled a tattoo of the 'Tree of Life'. The note also said that the dots were pierced one by one from the back of the mask so as not to tear the gold foil.

The case adjacent contained a bronze hinged item, a weapon belt, and a leather quiver decorated with gold. Moli read the notes: the bronze item had been used to connect a soldier's scabbard and his weapon belt and prevent the sheath from hitting his thigh when riding. These items were part of the Gold of the

Great Steppe Collection exhibited at the Fitzwilliam Museum in Cambridge.

Edith told her softly, "Morris once told me a legend regarding the Fitzwilliam Museum. At midnight, the stone lions outside the Museum would leave their posts and drink from Hobson's Conduit."

They moved to another display case with a few clay pots, cruses, some shells, some rolled golden microbeads sewn on boots, exquisite headdresses, and a small stone mill under a soft pale light. She read the accompanying note once again. These were objects found in a joint tomb that belonged to a Rouran general and a Rouran princess.

In another display case stood two red terracotta figurines, each about a metre tall, both quite chubby. They were dressed differently and had their hands on their chest as if they were bowing. The note informed Moli that it was uncommon to find statuettes this well preserved.

Next to the two figurines were camel figurines. These objects were found in the tomb of Princess Ruru, who had passed away when she was only eighteen years old. Two gold coins from the Byzantine Empire were also found in her tomb, along with a thousand pottery figurines.

Moli turned and saw a large screen with a map showing the changes in Rouran's territory. Another panel revealed the dining and clothing habits and some of the customs that the Rouran people followed.

Moli followed Edith to another glass case, where there were two metal beasts used as wine vessels. They were somewhat like bulldogs, but one had a few spikes on its back like a Stegosaurus and a pig's snout; the other had a body like a rhinoceros and the head of an ox, but its face had a shape like a star fruit.

She stared at the two stone beasts and thought that the ancient people had a remarkable imagination.

Why is it that the dragon is the only fictitious creature in the Chinese Zodiac?

Moli recalled that some researchers said that the image of the Chinese dragon came from ancient people's observation of crocodiles, compounded by a little imagination.

She thought about the dragons from *The Classic of Mountains and Seas.*

There was Zhulong or the illuminating dragon. The day breaks when it opens its eyes and sky falls when it closes them. There was Yinglong, a rare species of dragon that had wings and who had helped Yu the Great to treat the Yellow River's flooding.

Moli remembered a story that Edith had just told her about Nut, the sky goddess in Egyptian mythology who swallows the sun at night and gives birth to days.

Why is that the phoenix is a shared mythical creature in many cultures?

She followed Edith to another display case; there was an opened book that had many characters that Moli didn't know. She read the notes once again and found it to be a story from *The Book of Wei* – a classic text describing the history of the Northern Wei and Eastern Wei from the years 386 to 550 CE.

The story went like this:

'In Rouran, beliefs in shamanism prevailed. There was a young shamaness who staged a hoax to gain the appreciation of the Yujiulü Chounu Khan. She first kidnapped the Khan's younger brother. Then she told the Khan that the Tengri (the sky god) had apprehended his brother, but she could bring him back. The Khan and his mother were anxious to save his brother, and they followed the shamaness' instructions willingly. They set a large yurt as the shamaness instructed and she used ropes to descend the Khan's brother from the top of the tent to the ground. The Khan thought that the shamaness truly had supernatural powers and bestowed largesse on her.'

Moli followed Edith to the last display.

It was a stone pillar, its bottom sheared off. The top of the post had a carving of an animal's head. The animal had eyes like copper bells, whiskers like that of a catfish, two small horns, and inside its mouth there was something that looked like a handful of uncooked spaghetti.

Edith lowered her head and read the description.

"Excavated in the Junggar Basin in China in 1995. Use unknown, era unknown."

Could it be for tethering horses?

Moli examined the stone pillar and guessed. The last time she had visited her uncle and aunt, they'd taken a trip to the grasslands and, across springy turf, there were hitching posts intended to tether horses and to keep them from going astray.

She wished Morris could be there with her and tell her more about the Rourans' history.

Moli fixed her gaze on the animal on the stone pillar and wondered what animal had inspired such fantastic imagination from the ancients. For a second, she thought she saw the beast winking at her.

No way!

Moli took a breath and stared at the pillar for a long time, but nothing happened. She put her mind at ease, remembering Edith's theory about thinking as a library. Perhaps she'd let her imagination roam and it had gone to the wrong floor.

Chapter 4

Later, Edith took Moli to the café, hoping for a change in mood.

There were a few diners in the café, and Moli saw the Asian man from earlier eating a piece of cake. His date was not there, but her handbag stood on a chair, along with a few pamphlets on the Rouran exhibition. For some reason unknown to herself, Moli deliberately chose a table close to him. The man saw them and nodded lightly.

Edith was still disturbed. She stepped forward and said, "Listen, mister, I'm really sorry for what happened."

The man smiled. "Your apology is uncalled for."

Moli saw his umbrella leaning against the edge of the table, its handle a wood carving of a cat's head with glowing eyes.

Edith went to place their order, and Moli asked in Mandarin, "Do you know much about Rouran?" How she wished this man was one of Morris' colleagues, or even just an acquaintance.

"Not really...probably only as much as the exhibition tells," the man said. "But I grew up in Inner Mongolia, and I wanted to know more about Rouran."

Moli told him that her aunt and uncle also lived there.

"Sometimes, I miss living there very much." The man moved his plate as he spoke.

"Oh dearest..." His companion returned, and she sounded a little anxious. She leaned into the man's ear and said a few words.

The man nodded. "I'll go and buy some. Pads or tampons?"

"No. I think we better go back home." She approached Edith. "Sorry, umm...I was wondering if you might have any sanitary products with you?"

"You've found the right person to ask." Edith smiled. She took off her backpack, took out a packet of sanitary napkins and handed it to the woman.

"Oh! Thank you so much!"

"It's nuthin'," Edith replied warmly. "I have tampons if you need them."

The man thanked them while his date went to the washroom again. He introduced himself. His name was Chance Yang. He urged Edith to collect their beverages and join them on their table.

Moli introduced herself as well. She told Chance that 'mò lì' is pronounced as the same word as jasmine in Chinese.

"Please," Edith asked. "Could you...talk in English?"

"Yes, Aunt Edith." Moli nodded.

They talked about the exhibition for another minute or so, then Chance said, "Some historians say that some of the Rourans' descendants went to Italy. Some also say that the Rourans were linked with the Avars people."

"Italy?" Moli recalled. "The stone pillar with an animal's face carved onto it...there was spaghetti inside its mouth."

"Well, I have a slightly different theory," Chance said. "I think they might be strings."

"Like guitar strings?" Moli nodded. "That makes sense as well."

Chance took out a pen from his jacket pocket and wrote a word in Chinese on a napkin: 'Qiuniu'.

'Qiu' meant a prisoner and 'Niu' meant an ox.

"I know him!" Moli said. "Qiuniu is one of the dragon's nine sons."

"Yes." Chance put back his pen. "The nine sons of the dragon. Legend says that they each have their bailiwicks...specialities. Qiuniu is the dragon's eldest son and also the best-tempered one. It could distinguish the sounds of all things in the world; it had perfect pitch, so to speak. And Qiuniu liked to sit on musical instruments to enjoy the music." Chance paused. "My sister plays the Chinese lute, the *pipa*, and her teacher has always told her to play with effort so Qiuniu would help her to maintain her instrument."

"Do you know the other eight sons of the dragon?" Moli asked.

Chance furrowed his brow. "If you know, will you tell me them?"

"Of course." Moli sat up eagerly; her knowledge of dragons had finally come in handy.

"The second son of the dragon, Yazi, was aggressive and warlike, so people always carved its image on the handle of their weapons, especially swords. The third son was called Chaofeng, who liked high places, so they put it on the eaves and cornices of palaces or gar...goyles. The fourth one had a loud voice, and its image often appeared on clapperless bells. The fifth son looked like a lion. It was close with the Buddhas, so people had its image on incense burners. The dragon's sixth son was a giant turtle that could drink up three or four seas in one breath. To ensure the safety of ships, people put its image on bridges. The seventh son was a tiger who liked to meddle in human affairs, and people put its image on the doors of courts. The eighth son was fond of poetry and calligraphy, so people put it on stone tablets featuring notable works of famous writers. The youngest son was a fish with a large mouth. It could store water in its mouth and protect people from fires," Moli explained in one breath.

"Well," Chance mused. "What about Taotie? I always thought that was a son of the dragon as well."

Moli shrugged. "There are several versions of the nine sons of the dragon legend. Some say that the dragon had one greedy son called Taotie who was wont to eat fine food, and another called Pixiu who only eats but never poops."

"'Excrete' might be a better word," Chance said. "I know Pixiu. Merchants put its statue on their cash tills hoping only to have earnings and not expenses."

Moli thought about the stone pillar. "Do you think there might be eight other stone pillars for the other sons of the dragon?"

"We will leave that question to the archaeologists and the historians."

"My dad...he was a historian." Moli reluctantly used the past tense. "He organised this exhibition on Rouran. He passed away because of the virus."

Chance sighed. "We lost someone too...my wife's godfather."

The room seemed dreary all of a sudden.

He hesitated. "I read somewhere that cats have nine lives, Pac-Man three, and an isotope only half a life, but it lasts a long time. I have lost others too, but my ability to bear pain has not grown. Someone told me that there is no learning curve for pain. Sticks and stones break bones, and names and words will hurt. Bruises can heal, and scars can fade, but the wounds inside hearts rankle the most. People simply have no imagination for pain."

Moli wondered if people felt pain the same way.

"I hope I didn't set a bad example for you." Chance smiled faintly. "If you run into a situation like this, walk away. Ignore them. Just because you don't say anything back, it doesn't mean that you are a coward, or that you're at a disadvantage. Your safety is the most important thing. Apologies work, and so do the police. The more flawed someone's reasoning, the louder their shouting, the higher they raise their fists. Fish have a memory that lasts more than seven seconds, but a human?" Chance looked at his umbrella. "I always tell myself: don't think too badly of people and don't think too highly of them either. Especially don't take too much of what others say to heart. It wouldn't do to let others define me for me, right?"

His wife had returned. She introduced herself as Catherine. Moli and Edith chatted with them for a while. Catherine was a florist, but her shop had been closed for some time. Chance worked as a consultant. They have a one-and-a-half-year-old girl called Lasa.

Edith found out that she and Catherine had had the same professor of English literature and history. Catherine also had a ginger cat, called Mr Darcy, who had recently been on an unsuccessful diet.

"Thank you so much," Catherine said to Edith once again.

"I say that many friendships start with one borrowing pads and tampons from another." Edith smiled sheepishly. "I think we should learn from Scotland, where they provide them free of charge. And there's still so much taboo talking about menstruation. I wish we would talk about menstruation as if we're talking about the weather."

Catherine agreed. "Yes...and all those commercials. They're so irrelevant and outdated. Who would wear white trousers during their period and run barefoot on the beach? I doubt if any of these companies did any market research."

Edith nodded. "I and some friends from uni started a social impact project aiming to provide free sanitary products to the homeless in Lon—" she said as her phone vibrated. Edith checked her phone; there was a message from Maggie.

"Moli. Your mother said her company needs her to stay for a few more days. She asked me to take you to the hotel they've arranged."

They finished their tea and juice and said goodbye to Chance and Catherine.

Before parting, Moli felt the eyes of the cat on Chance's umbrella handle had become greener.

***

That evening, Moli lay on the bed in her hotel room, headphones on, video chatting with her grandparents. Edith sat on the sofa in the room, checking her phone while watching TV.

"Hate crimes on the streets of London are on the rise..." the news anchor said wearily.

Edith changed the channel. But *Strictly Come Dancing* came on, and she turned the TV off.

She charged her phone, stood up, and walked to the window. Very few lights in the office buildings around Holborn; very few cars on the streets; very few people passing under her window.

The only thing that was in excess was sorrow and sadness.

Edith leaned against the window, not knowing what to do.

Moli had told her earlier that "at school, we learnt how to write birthday cards in English, we learnt how to write diaries in English, we learnt how to write emails and reports in English, but no one taught us what to do about discrimination in English."

'I sense that you are weighed down by the white man's burden.'

Edith recalled that man's words and sighed.

She had been to Shanghai. But she didn't know about Maggie's family, didn't know Moli's city, let alone China. She also didn't know England or London, let alone her county's parish-pump politics, that well.

Probably no one but Donald Trump would claim to be an expert on so many subjects...

Edith had tried to play her role as an aunt today, but still. There were moments, when she did nothing, when that woman shouted, she could have said something.

If Moli hadn't been there, Edith thought she might have quickly escaped from that scene as if it were none of her business. Listening to Moli's conversation with that man, she felt he had accomplished a task that she had failed.

If countries were imagined communities, then we had imagined our own country, and also imagined the other countries, Edith thought.

What are we to believe? What do we want to believe? What is made up for us to believe? And who are those who encouraged us to accuse and to forget selectively? Who gains from post-truth politics?

Some people thought that 5G networks could spread the virus; others believed that the Earth was flat. There were people who died from COVID and who had still denied the virus until the very last moment.

Imagination is a powerful and scary thing.

Do our values influence our thinking? Or does our thinking distort our values?

Edith didn't know and, for a moment, she thought it didn't matter. But on second thoughts, she couldn't stop thinking about it.

Rouran...

Edith mumbled the word. It sounded ancient and distant.

Only after seeing the exhibition had she realised that the Rouran Dynasty took place after the Three Kingdoms.

The Qin, Han, Ming, and Qing dynasties...

If it weren't for Morris, she wouldn't have been able to place them on a timeline.

Edith often watched Li Ziqi's videos, but she couldn't remember the last time she had read a book by a Chinese author or listened to a Chinese singer. At university, when it came to Chinese films, they still only played *To Live*.

Perhaps the speed of imagination is much faster than our rate of perception and comprehension.

Edith thought about Fluffy, Hua's cat. Someone had dumped its body into their garden with the word "VIRUS" written on its belly in yellow paint.

Perhaps people also face the problem of time inconsistency in their thinking, knowing that they have to look at things rationally, but still letting that irrational, biased self come up on top. Will they ever regret and repent for being aggressive when there was no evidence, and reluctant to offer an apology even when they knew they were wrong?

"Aunt Edith?" Moli called.

"Yes?" Edith turned back. "Would you like something to eat?"

"Maggie said she's still in a meeting and she'll be back later. She's having a great time with 'strategy'," Moli joked.

Edith checked her phone. "I know we had dinner early. How would you like some flapjacks?"

"Too much sugar is probably not good," Moli mused, "but why not?"

They had some flapjacks as a snack, then Moli showered and Edith helped her to dry her hair.

Later, Moli busied herself with some maths homework on the bed while Edith sat beside her, reading a book.

Having completed the worksheet, Moli put down her pencil. "Aunt Edith, what are you reading?"

"Some poems." Edith showed them to her.

"*Ariel* by Sylvia Plath," Moli read. She thought for a while. "Aunt Edith, when I go back home, I'm going to send you some Chinese poetry. I think you'll like it." She paused. "Aunt Edith, why don't you learn Mandarin?"

Edith bookmarked her reading and put the book on her lap. "Because it is rather hard to learn. It's no use being able to read the *pinyin* without knowing the meaning of the characters, and it's no use memorising the characters but not knowing how to pronounce them." She wondered, "Moli, can you tell me more about your city?"

"Sure." Moli sat up. "My city is called Penglai. It belongs to the city of Yantai; 'yān tái' originally meant a beacon tower where people made smoke to notify the guards of attacking enemies. It's a small, coastal city and it's close to Qingdao. Most people know Qingdao because it's famous for its beer. Qingdao was once ceded to Germany."

"And what is your city famous for?"

Moli counted with her fingers. "Beaches, apples, cherries, and pears. And seafood. Oh! And the Penglai Pavilion! Legend says it's a place where gods and immortals lived. And it's famous for mirages, though I've never seen one. Aunt Edith, did you know the first emperor of Qin Dynasty, Qin Shi Huang, wanted to find...wait, let me check the word." She quickly typed something on her phone. "Umm...he wanted to find the elixir of immortality, and he ordered a man called Xu Fu to find it."

"And what was the elixir?" Edith asked.

"Hmm. According to legends...it's some kind of...wait, let me check again. Ah. They were looking for the alkahest... But my grandmother once said that the elixir to immortality is *taisui*."

"And what is a 'taisui'?"

"My grandma says it's a meaty creature that looks like flesh. I have a book called *The Classic of Mountains and Seas* that has an entry on it. If people slice off a portion, it will grow back again."

Moli typed something on her phone and handed it to Edith. She took it and read off the screen: "Taisui is a complex of bacteria, fungi, and myxomycete whose extracts may contain anticarcinogenic and antioxidant properties."

Moli shrugged. "Xu Fu sailed with his retinue from Penglai but was never heard from again. Historians say he could have landed in Japan. Oh! Penglai is also famous for wine!"

"Wine?"

"Yes. During the Second Opium War, when the Anglo-French troops occupied Yantai in 1860, they discovered a large patch of wild grapes that they used to make wine. Later, a Chinese businessman decided to set up a winery there. Its wine was so famous that even Mr Sun Yat-sen praised it highly."

Edith nodded. "You know a lot about your city."

"Well... My grandpa always says that never to forget history. I think I know very little about Mexican history and Western people know very little about Chinese history." Moli paused. "Aunt Edith, what does 'blotto lar...gato' mean? Is it a bad word?"

"Well... it means to get very drunk very slowly," Edith explained. "It's not a bad word. Maybe more of a state of mind."

Moli asked again, "And what is a...slag? Or is it slug?"

Edith did not correct her this time. "Well, a slug is a creature like a snail without the shell."

"I see," Moli nodded understandingly. "I like to walk near the shore. We have many seashells. And there is a big whale, an art project, not far from where we live." Moli tilted her head. "Aunt Edith, how about if I teach you Chinese? I have a very nice way to learn languages. Association. We can start with simple words. If you learn a word a day, you will learn many in a year. See, you just taught me a word now."

She settled herself comfortably on the bed. "We can start from today. Let me think. How about the word 'lǎo tiě'? It's like 'old bean' in English. 'Lǎo tiě' means that the friendship between two people is as strong as steel and iron."

"Lǎo...tiě." Edith repeated the word. "I will remember." She tucked Moli in. "You can teach me another word tomorrow morning."

"Yeah." Moli closed her eyes. "Tomorrow...I will teach you a word about cats. It's 'māo zhǎng fēng'," she murmured. "Good night, Aunt Edith. You can guess what it means for now."

"Good night, Moli. Sweet dreams," Edith said as she dimmed the bedside lamp.

***

Sometime later, the doorbell rang.

Moli opened her eyes slowly. She didn't know how long she had been asleep for, but there was no light coming through under the curtains. It was probably still night-time.

The doorbell continued to ring.

Moli had never heard a doorbell like this; not the usual 'ding-dong', but a piece of music.

She yawned and sat up, looking around.

Did Aunt Edith forget to turn off the TV?

She lifted the blanket, put on her slippers, and got out of bed.

It was a little chilly in the room so Moli put on her coat as well.

Aunt Edith rolled over and slept soundly.

♪♪ ♪♪ ♪♪

Moli found the TV; the black screen reflected her silhouette.

Suddenly, her reflection disappeared.

Numerous colourful waves danced on the screen to the sound of the doorbell.

Must be a dream...

Moli remembered. *Or Maggie is ringing the bell. Of course. That's it! She didn't have a key card.*

Moli walked to the door; she was not tall enough to check the peephole.

"Mom?" she asked.

No answer.

Edith had locked the door chain. Moli wondered if she should open the door to see who was behind it.

The doorbell still rang.

♪ ♪ ♪♪ ♪♪

Her hand found the doorknob in the darkness.

It was cold.

She felt the coldness of the metal. And something odd...

Like...scales...

Like...snakeskin...

The doorknob moved!

Moli was startled and jumped back.

"Do forgive me for calling on you uninvited," a rich voice rumbled.

Moli took a deep breath. There was a small animal standing on the doorknob.

"Yet how can a dream without music be called a 'sweet dream'?"

A small lantern lit up above the animal's head.

Moli closed her eyes, took another deep breath, and opened her eyes again.

The music stopped.

She stared at the doorknob. It was just a doorknob.

"Quite a close call," the voice continued. "Almost missed a note..."

Moli spun around. The animal was sitting on the TV, its head emitting a pale-yellow light.

It was as tall as the small fridge in the room, with a face of a Chinese alligator, two small horns like a calf, and long, thin whiskers like a dragon's.

"Shall I introduce myself again?" it inquired.

Moli swallowed. Her eyes told her that Qiuniu was in her room. Her brain told her that was impossible.

"In case you were wondering, dragons do speak human languages."

No way! Moli shouted in her head.

The music changed.

She saw the animal carried a miniature *guqin* of a sort, a plucked seven-string Chinese musical instrument.

"Do these strings still favour noodles?" Qiuniu asked as it played a few notes. They were crisp and pleasing to the ear.

This can't be...this can't be...this can't be...this can't be...this can't be...

Moli stood there.

"A lie repeated a thousand times is still not the truth, yet the same note played a thousand times may become a tune." Qiuniu floated up towards Moli. "What would you say?"

Moli's hands were shaking, her throat dry, her head dizzy, and her legs wanted to run away. She understood how Lord Ye felt now.

"When my cousin paid a visit to Lord Ye, he was so scared that he piddled." Qiuniu showed its crocodile-like teeth, probably laughing. "Follow me. Please."

Its green eyes disappeared.

Moli stood still.

There was nothing amiss in the room.

Edith snored a little. Some small sounds of electricity passed through the ceiling.

What a dream...

Moli suppressed a yawn.

No wonder people often say that you dream what you think about daily.

She found a bottle of mineral water on the small table in the room and had a mouthful.

"Follow me..." Qiuniu's voice said again.

The remaining water inside whirled like a musical fountain.

Not a dream...

Moli felt lost. The adults always told her not to talk to strangers offline and online, but they didn't say anything about not talking to strange dragons.

A warm bed was just a few steps away, and Moli could get under the blanket, close her eyes, pretend nothing had happened, and go home with Maggie in a few days.

Moli approached the bed.

Or...

She quietly picked up her jumper and trousers. And found her sneakers.

"Lao...tie," Edith muttered.

Moli pulled the blanket over Edith and left. She moved a chair to the door, got up, unleashed the security chain, and gently turned the doorknob.

Chapter 5

The door opened.

Moli did not know where to turn.

It was the same hallway, the same carpet, the same walls painted in warm green.

Someone was watching football in the room next door.

Moli looked to her right then to her left.

Qiuniu was nowhere to be seen.

♪~ ♪~ ♪~

Music.

She could hear music.

Moli followed the sound to the lift. She was just about to call the lift.

'Ding dong!' The lift door opened.

"Follow me."

Moli entered the lift.

There were mirrors inside, in which she saw countless reflections of herself.

Moli remembered that the ghost from the Korean horror movie hid in a lift to haunt people. But she was not scared anymore.

The music continued.

The floor buttons inside the lift were like the buttons on an accordion. They flickered and shone to the rhythm of the music.

"Ground floor," the lift informed her.

Moli put on her mask, pulled up the zipper of her coat, and stepped into the hotel lobby.

No one was in sight, but the piano in the bar played by itself as if a cat were tap-dancing on the keyboard.

"Follow me."

No one was at the front desk. Moli quickly ran to the entrance.

Once outside, she saw Qiuniu perched on top of a traffic light not far to her right.

The music had changed again.

Moli knew that tune. Her uncle would sometimes play it on the guitar.

It was called *Recuerdos de la Alhambra*.

The pedestrian crossing became an audio equaliser displaying the rhythm.

"Did Zhuangzi dream of the butterfly. Or did the butterfly dream of Zhuangzi?"

Qiuniu finished playing and bowed. "Follow me."

"Where to?" Moli asked.

"To where you need to go and to where you are needed."

The crosswalk calmed, and the green light stayed on.

Moli examined her surroundings.

No cars. No people.

She gingerly crossed the road, her feet making a sound with each step.

A door appeared in front of Moli. A most ordinary wooden door.

"Follow me." Qiuniu led the way.

It was dark inside. She couldn't even see her own fingers.

"Light up," Qiuniu said.

Torches lit up one by one on the stone walls.

"This is the Corridor of War," Qiuniu explained. "There is no virus here."

She took off her mask and pocketed it.

The dank stone-flagged corridor was long and filled with damp, earthy air. Every few steps there was a large bolted door with a handwheel on its side.

Moli wondered what was behind these doors.

"Well..." She remembered the ice breakers she had learnt, but now was not a good time to talk about the weather. Instead, she asked in a shaky voice, "If dragons do exist, why don't you save people?"

Qiuniu replied, "Humans make history. We only remember." The rutilant light emitting from its body became more dazzling. "There have been as many plagues as wars in history, yet plagues and wars take people equally by surprise. It seems that humans are once again in the grip of an extraordinarily dangerous outbreak of forgetfulness."

Moli looked at the doors on either side of her. Images emerged on their surfaces.

"This is the Nagorno-Karabakh conflict," Qiuniu said.

"This is the War in Donbas," Qiuniu said.

"This is the Invasion of Iraq," Qiuniu said.

"This is the Gulf War," Qiuniu said.

"This is the Vietnam War," Qiuniu said.

"This is the Korean War," Qiuniu said.

"This is the Algerian War," Qiuniu said.

"This is the Chinese Civil War," Qiuniu said.

"This is the Atomic bombings of Hiroshima and Nagasaki," Qiuniu said.

"This is the Nanjing Massacre," Qiuniu said.

"This is the Pearl Harbor Attack," Qiuniu said.

"This is the Holocaust," Qiuniu said.

"This is the Blitz," Qiuniu said.

"This is the Porajmos," Qiuniu said.

"This is the Irish War of Independence," Qiuniu said.

"This is the Armenian Genocide," Qiuniu said.

"This is the Russo–Japanese War," Qiuniu said.

"This is the Eight-Nation Alliance," Qiuniu said.

"This is the Butcher of Congo," Qiuniu said.

"This is the Town Destroyer..." Qiuniu said.

Moli was silent.

The corridor extended to countless doors. She didn't know how long it was, but she felt as though she had walked for miles.

"Are you weary?" Qiuniu asked.

"A little," Moli confessed.

So many wars. So many lives lost.

She was tired and disheartened.

"Allow me." Qiuniu struck the strings on the *guqin* a few times and conjured up a cloud that was the size of Grandpa Orozco's pastry board.

"Please," Qiuniu gestured her to climb up the cloud. "We still have quite a distance to cover."

Moli touched the cloud. It felt like a cushion, and not cool at all. "Wow!"

She climbed on top. "Is this the Monkey King's cloud?" She felt around. "Magic does exist!" she exclaimed.

"What you might think as magic, we consider as science," Qiuniu said. "And sometimes there is a difference between real science and what humans believe to be science."

"Science..." Moli murmured.

"Yes. Science." Qiuniu pondered, "Why do you think that the Monkey King survived the Grand Supreme Elder Lord's alchemy finery after forty-nine days? You know the story, right? The Monkey King was sentenced to be melted into water in that furnace for creating havoc in the Sky Palace and wounding a hundred thousand warriors."

"Well," Moli thought, "because...he...his body was made of stone?"

"Quite right." Qiuniu nodded. "Siliceous rocks consist mainly or entirely of silicon dioxide with a melting point of 1,610°C."

"And the furnace? How hot could it be?"

"It employed a rather obsolete combustion system design that could only reach 1,200°C."

Moli felt a penny had dropped.

It made sense!

She had yet to learn chemistry at school, but she felt truly astounded.

"And this cloud is not the Monkey King's cloud. He would not have lent it to us." Qiuniu smiled and added, "This is a digital cloud and we call it Eniac."

"Digital cloud?"

"It makes use of digital data. Behold." Qiuniu landed on the cloud and lifted a tiny corner with its claw.

Moli leaned close. She saw a display with two lines of numbers.

1 - 5473

0 - 372

The two numbers after "1" and "0" decreased gradually.

"This digital cloud consumes data from the Web of All Things. Facts glow well, and lies give a slow burn," Qiuniu explained as the cloud carried Moli further down the Corridor of War.

After a while, the cloud halted in front of a door.

Qiuniu plucked the strings once again. The door opened, and inside was an ancient-style hall.

"After you," Qiuniu said.

Moli hopped down from the digital cloud and stepped onto the grey stone floor.

"What is this place?" she asked tentatively.

"This is the Hall of Ten Thousand Sages."

"If I go in, will I age when I come out again?" Moli asked, perturbed. She remembered a legend that said 'one day in the immortal world meant ten years spent in the human world'.

"Rest assured. This is the...realm."

"I'm sorry. The what realm?" Moli asked.

"This is the realm of π. You are safe here. Nonetheless, never attempt to enter the imaginary realm. If any human entered the imaginary realm, all worlds should perish." Qiuniu continued, "The Tao produced One; One produced Two; Two produced Three; Three produced all things."

"Then you'd better tell me which doors to stay away from," Moli said cautiously.

"There are two doors emblazoned with the letter 'i', denoting humans' self-interest," Qiuniu said. "Never go near them. When both doors open, the Tao ceases to exist."

Moli made a mental note to watch out for doors with the letter 'i'.

If you multiply two imaginary numbers, i, you get minus one. Does this have anything to do with the imaginary realm? she wondered.

After a few seconds, Moli finally decided to enter the hall.

She saw a scroll hanging below the wood cross-beams, but there was nothing on it.

"Brother, wherefore to bring a human child home?" A thundering voice came from above as if someone had turned the stereo on at full blast in Moli's head.

She looked up. There was a hammock hanging in between the rafters.

A pony's tail fell out, except its colour was seaweed green.

The tail swung once, twice, and retracted.

This must be Pulao, the one who likes to roar, so people put its image on bells, Moli thought.

"So she could have a sweet dream."

Moli turned and discovered that Qiuniu had grown. It was as big as a calf now.

Qiuniu sat down on an antique chair, still holding the antique *guqin.*

Moli settled on another chair.

She looked around and saw Pulao's tail swaying in mid-air, teasing the digital cloud.

"Why is this place called the 'Hall of Ten Thousand Sages' and not...the Hall of Nine Immortals?" Moli asked while waiting. "I don't remember there were so many entries in *The Classic of Mountains and Seas.*"

Qiuniu plucked a note. "Moli, do you know about the five kingdoms?"

"The five kingdoms?" Moli shrugged. "I know about the Three Kingdoms. I've watched many documentaries about it."

"Well. Human scientists use the five kingdoms to classify all living things. So first, you have the Animal and the Plant Kingdoms. Then you have the Monera Kingdom, consisting of single-celled organisms that have no true nucleus like bacteria. Then there is the Fungi Kingdom and the Protist Kingdom, which consists of anything that is not a plant, a fungus, or an animal."

"I know what a fungus is," Moli exclaimed. "A *taisui* is a fungus."

Qiuniu only smiled and nodded. "Other than the five kingdoms, human scientists also use phyla, classes, and orders to categorise all living organisms. For instance, humans belong to the Hominidae family. And in the realm of π, every sage oversees a Family and hence the Hall of Ten Thousand Sages—"

"Oh! Why isn't Father back yet?"

A zircon blue-striped tiger rushed through the door. It did not seem to mind Moli's presence. The tiger lay down on the ground like a relaxed cat, exposing its fuzzy belly.

Bi'an, the meddlesome one.

Moli observed the tiger.

"I'm seventh in the line," the tiger said lazily. "Umm...why don't you do me a favour? There has been a dispute that I can't figure out. Perhaps you might judge it differently."

"Umm... sure," Moli said.

Bi'an stood up on all four paws. "There is someone whose old mother is very ill. He has no money to get medicine, so he robbed the clinic. What should his sentence be?"

"Well, if it is a petty crime then perhaps you could extend him some credit so he could pay back the money over time?"

"I see." Bi'an nodded, its whiskers moving up and down. "Then there is a man whose old mother is very ill, and he has no money for medicine, so he steals the medicine from another villager's house. The villager's child is rather sick. What should this man's sentence be?"

"If they don't drink the medicine on time are the consequences bad?"

"There is a man whose old mother is very ill, so he steals the medicine from another villager's house, causing the young child to pass away. What should this man's sentence be?"

"He...he saved his mother's life, but..."

"There is now a doctor who has enough medicine but only for one patient. Is it money or ethics that comes first?"

"Can't we find a better way to save them both?"

"There is a city where the citizens are ill, and medical supplies scarce, so the chief robbed a neighbouring city. What is your judgement?"

Moli was momentarily speechless.

"What if there is a city where the citizens are ill, and medical supplies scarce, so the chief robbed a neighbouring town. But he didn't distribute them equitably among his people; instead, the highest bidders got them. What is your verdict then? Is it money or social responsibility that comes first? One race suffers more than another, is one life not worth saving than another?"

"To borrow someone's words, 'no, I wouldn't say so, but perhaps that's been the story of life'," Pulao interrupted loudly. Its orotund voice resounded for several moments. "And certainly, as someone noted, 'not all deaths are equal, for you cannot call every death a tragedy. A tragedy is when a child dies. A tragedy is when some young woman or young man dies, or when someone in their middle years dies. But are you not diminishing a life so well lived if you call it a tragedy when someone at eighty or ninety meets their mortality?' If one savoured the last part of their life in a citadel or a garth in a high castle fenced by ramparts and bulwarks, some for sure would think of it as a relief, a reward; a blessing, even."

"Shouldn't people seek an explanation from those who have taken a crisis and turned it into tragedies? It is always better safe than sorry."

"Bi'an, have you forgotten the tale of the 'fiend with one eye and five bodies' so quickly?"

"What was it about?" Moli asked. She had never heard such a story.

The hammock shook as Pulao explained. "The 'fiend with one eye and five bodies' was a tale from Yuan Mei's book *What the Master Would Not Discuss*. You know Yuan Mei, right? He was a scholar from Qing Dynasty who liked to collect supernatural sightings. And by 'Master', we are not talking about some *seigneurs* and feudal lords, but Confucius. The story has it that the 'fiend with one eye and five bodies' would often appear in the unfortunate years with pandemics. The fiend consists of five ghosts, but only one has an eye, so the other four would blindly follow the leading ghost's instructions. They performed their devilry by catching the scent of humans one by one. If the first ghost caught a sniff of someone, that person would fall ill. If the second, third, and fourth ghosts continue to inhale, that person's state of health would deteriorate further. If the fifth ghost, that is, the leading ghost with one eye, sniffed, then that person died. It was rumoured that one night, a lodger in an inn overheard how the fiend harmed humans. He lay awake that night and heard the leading ghost saying, 'that man is a man of virtue, do not harm him'. Then later, he heard the leading ghost again, saying, 'this man is a blessed man, do not hurt him either'. Then later, the lodger listened to the leading ghost talking again, 'that man is a ruffian, do not provoke him either'. Then the other four ghosts asked whom they should have for supper, and the lodger heard the leading ghost saying, 'you shall sniff these two; these are the most ordinary persons. They have done nothing superbly good and nothing awfully wrong. No one will care if they die'."

"But shouldn't one extend the respect of the aged in his family to that of other families and the love of the young ones in his family to that of other families? I still can't figure it out. The humans, that is." The tiger shook its head and stared at the blank scroll.

Moli turned. A painting had appeared on the scroll. She didn't know the name of the painting, but she did know that it was a work by Leonardo da Vinci. There was a naked man, with four arms and four legs, standing in a square and a circle.

"I wonder if trying to achieve equity and equality would be as difficult as trying to square the circle," Bi'an sighed. "What do you think? Suanni?"

"A Bodhisattva should forsake dharmas, still more so no-dharmas." A gentle voice filled the room.

"What is 'dharma'?" Moli lowered her voice and asked Qiuniu.

"The teachings of the Buddha," Qiuniu replied.

"Let us focus on the present moment," the gentle voice said.

Moli felt as if a piece of fine jade had drifted into her ears and her heart itched as if a dragonfly had dabbed its tail in a lotus pond, suffusing out ripples.

A scent came, comfortable and soporific.

"Ah... You've lit that agarwood incense again. It makes my eyes heavy." Bi'an lay down and purred like a cat while Qiuniu played the rhythm of 'High Mountains and Flowing Water' with gusto.

Moli drifted into sleep...

Chapter 6

BOOM, BOOM, BOOM.

Large drums sounded in the distance.

Moli bounced up in fright.

"Ahhhhhhh!" Pulao shrieked, its screams as loud as an explosion.

Moli saw Pulao twitching in the hammock as if it had had an electric shock. It was only then that she saw Pulao in full. It had antlers, a leopard's head, and a teal complexion.

"Whale alert!" Bi'an, the blue tiger, flitted into the air like a fast arrow. "Must Yazi always borrow trouble?"

Whoosh! A fireball landed in the courtyard.

Sparks, splinters, and segments of rocks splattered everywhere. Out of reflex, Moli shielded her head with her arms. Then something chafed her right hand.

A sharp pang of pain seared her.

BOOM! BOOM! BOOM! BOOM! BOOM!

The drumming intensified.

"Enemy!" Bi'an shouted. "War elephants, no less than a thousand!"

"Owwww! Someone! Stop that whale!" Pulao continued to scream. Moli worried that it might yank down the cross-beams and collapse the hall.

"Do not panic!" Qiuniu grabbed its *guqin* and plinked a piece *prestissimo*. The digital cloud hid behind Qiuniu as the music flowed; Pulao seemed to have calmed down.

"Bi'an! Go and scout where the enemy has advanced! Suanni, you take care of Pulao!" Qiuniu plucked another fast-tempo song. "Moli, it seems that I have invited you at a bad time."

BOOMMMM! BOOMMMM! BOOMMMM! More drumbeats at a different pitch.

"AARRRGGHHH!" Pulao went berserk. It overturned the roof, roaring up into the clouds.

"The enemy's drum is made from the skin of Yinglong!" Bi'an shouted. "How spiteful to attack us with our own kind!"

"Don't panic!"

Moli saw Qiuniu plucking the strings of the *guqin* so quickly that its claws trembled.

"AARRRGGHHH!" Pulao crashed onto the roof.

"Pulao is losing it!"

A barrage of fire and spall exploded around Moli. She saw Bi'an fall like a feather into the rubble.

"Suanni, take her and go!" Qiuniu ordered.

"But, brother!" Suanni demurred.

"This is no time to think. ACT NOW!" At these words, a string broke on Qiuniu's *guqin*.

A searing wave of air knocked Moli over.

"There is no alternative..." she heard Qiuniu whine.

Moli opened her eyes. Qiuniu snapped a piece of string from its *guqin* and handed it to her.

"The string will help! GO! NOW!" Qiuniu's body brightened.

"Follow me!" Suanni led Moli through the door and into the Corridor of War. It was a fiery red lion with phoenix-like claws and a mane of fire.

"Forgive me, but I'm worried about my brothers," Suanni admitted. "The digital cloud shall see you home."

"Please be careful!" Moli climbed up the cloud and urged the red lion.

The digital cloud carried her through the Corridor of War as fast as a rollercoaster.

Moli could still hear the sounds of bombing and roaring behind her.

A dream could never be so vivid...

Her heart pounded.

She had so many questions that buzzed in her head.

Who were the attackers? Were dragons not invincible? Could dragons die?

She remembered Bi'an's cry, "The enemy's drum is made from the skin of Yinglong! How spiteful to attack us with our own kind!"

Who could be powerful enough to skin Yinglong?

The Corridor of War seemed endless.

Moli looked around. She had reached the medieval part now.

A hollow silence like a vacuum.

Moli could only hear her breathing and heartbeat.

She felt pain in her right palm. When she looked down, she found a deep cut that was still bleeding.

Not a dream.

Her pain was real. Her fear was real.

Suddenly, a voice like a long-running creek echoed in the corridor.

"Who is't that dare trespass..."

"Who is't that dare..."

"Who is't that..."

"Who is't..."

"Who..."

Moli held her breath, not daring to make a sound. She looked at the doors flying past her; she was in the World Wars section now.

Faster! Moli pleaded.

"Who is't that dare trespass the Corridor of War?"

The echoes neared by the second.

Moli looked up, and her mouth gaped.

Oh my...

Something had blocked her way.

It was a grand tortoise the size of a tank, with a giant serpent, as wide as a barrel of gasoline, wrapped around its body.

The snake hissed, and the tortoise stomped.

Seeing is believing. This is Xuanwu.

"Who," the giant serpent hissed.

"Is't," the grand tortoise rumbled.

"That dare," the giant serpent sibilated.

"Trespass," the grand tortoise bellowed.

"I am not *trespassing*!" Moli couldn't stand the torment. "Qiuniu brought me here."

"Oh?" the grand tortoise inquired.

"Oh," the giant serpent noted.

More silence.

"Did Qiuniu bring you here?" the grand tortoise asked.

"Qiuniu brought you here, did it not?" the giant serpent added.

"The sons of the dragon are under attack. Please go and help them!" Moli implored.

"Is Qiuniu above the law?" the grand tortoise asked.

"Above the law, is it?" the giant serpent repeated.

"Or is Qiuniu below the law?" the grand tortoise asked.

"Below the law, is it?" the giant serpent repeated.

"Let me pass! Please!" Moli urged.

"Is Qiuniu above or below the law?" the grand tortoise asked.

"Qiuniu is neither above nor below the law," the giant serpent replied.

Moli panicked. She now knew that she should never talk to a strange dragon.

"And Qiuniu breached the law..." the grand tortoise rumbled.

"Breached the law, it did," the giant serpent confirmed.

Moli felt centuries had passed since she had got out of her bed that night.

"Unless..." the grand tortoise muttered.

"Lest..." the giant serpent hissed.

"Answer two questions," the grand tortoise advised.

"We might let you go," the giant serpent whistled.

"What questions?" Moli took a deep breath. She wondered if all mythical creatures had inquisitive minds.

"There is a number," the grand tortoise chanted.

"If it is an odd number," the giant serpent intoned.

"Multiply it by three then plus one," the grand tortoise said.

"If it is even," the giant serpent added.

"Divide it by two," the grand tortoise commanded.

"And so it goes," the giant serpent hissed.

"A hundred times," the grand tortoise rumbled.

"You shall have the truth," the giant serpent declared.

"What is that number?" the grand tortoise and the giant serpent asked together.

Moli was puzzled. "What do you mean by the 'truth'?"

"There is only one truth," the grand tortoise voiced.

"And the truth is always one," the giant serpent offered.

There is a number...

Moli's head spun.

If it is an odd number, you multiply it by three then add one; if it's an even number, you divide it by two; you repeat the process for the new result for a hundred times, then you get one eventually.

Moli vaguely recalled her Maths teacher mentioning something called a 'hailstone sequence' in class.

There was a 'magical' natural number.

Twenty... It was over twenty, she recalled.

"You have our undivided attention," the grand tortoise said.

"Our undivided attention, you have," the giant serpent repeated.

"Please, the answer," the grand tortoise demanded.

"The answer, please," the giant serpent insisted.

"Twenty-three. No. Twenty-seven?" Moli offered tentatively.

Xuanwu moved slowly towards her.

"Wrong?" the grand tortoise queried.

"Right," the giant serpent confirmed.

Moli breathed a big, big sigh of relief.

"Next question," the grand tortoise said.

"Question that follows," the giant serpent said.

"Does P equal NP?" the grand tortoise asked.

"Or does it not?" the giant serpent added.

Moli had not the slightest idea of what they were asking.

"Is it a big picture that is easy to follow?" the grand tortoise asked.

"Or is it the minor details that are hard to mellow?" the giant serpent added.

"Are major dilemmas easy to solve?" the grand tortoise pondered.

"Or are small puzzles difficult to convolve?" the giant serpent wondered.

"Do you know aught about your world? We are all ears..." they voiced jointly.

Oh my!

Moli watched as they stepped closer and closer.

"All ears we are," Xuanwu announced.

"Go! Go! Go!" Moli shouted to the digital cloud.

It carried her flying backwards.

"Do you want to escape the tortoise and fall to the snake?" Xuanwu voiced.

Moli covered her ears, not daring to listen any further. But she felt the digital cloud was shrinking every second.

At first, she could sit on it, then only kneel on it, and finally only crouch on it.

Moli checked the display. Now there were only single digits left after the '1' and '0'.

She jumped off the cloud and rolled onto the rocky ground. The cloud made a noise and shrank to the size of a wireless mouse's USB receiver.

Moli pocketed it and she ran.

"Escape the tortoise..." that voice echoed again.

"And fall to the snake..."

No way!

Moli looked ahead. Unknowingly, she was besieged by the grand tortoise and the giant serpent.

How is this possible!

After tonight, everything was possible.

Moli laughed at herself.

What to do?

She could not advance, nor could she retreat.

There was a door not far away. She wondered which war it was. Moli ran to the door and managed to turn the handwheel. The door opened a crack.

'Never near the two doors emblazoned with the letter "i".' She remembered how Qiuniu had warned her.

Moli checked the door. Her fingers felt a small protrusion. She was not sure if it was an 'i' or an 'l'. Moli did not dare to risk it.

"Escape the tortoise and fall to the snake."

Xuanwu approached.

No.

Xuan and Wu approached.

Moli shut the door and looked around.

She could not dare to venture from the snake's side, but the tortoise...

Then Moli remembered that her grandpa had always said that turtles bite hard.

At that moment, Moli felt a vibration in her coat pocket. It was Qiuniu's broken string. A sharp light blurred her vision. Something furry...and a tail brushed against her hand.

"Feiiii!" a voice shrilled.

When Moli opened her eyes again, she was still in the Corridor of War.

Xuanwu was far behind her. The giant serpent had coiled on top of the grand tortoise, chasing after her.

"Flee...no...more!" they shouted in unison.

Moli did not know what was happening. There was a door in front of her, and she checked it frantically. It had a smooth surface. She opened the door just enough for her to get in.

"Flee...no...more..."

Moli had no time to think further. She squeezed in. Then Moli saw the universe.

And galaxies...

She wondered how Yuri Gagarin had felt when he first saw the curvature of the Earth.

Her uncle told her once that the taikonauts at the Tiangong space station could see sixteen sunrises and sixteen sunsets every day. Moli marvelled at the sight in front of her. But there was no space junk, nor satellite, nor space stations.

All of a sudden, Moli felt a force dragging her. The force grew stronger and stronger, pulling her. She was scared that she might drift into the universe or into a black hole.

Nooooooo!

That was her last thought before she fell.

Chapter 7

*T*iansu got up before dawn. He dressed, whet his knife blade, and made to leave in the wan dawn light. Although he had not yet qualified as a solider, he followed the schedule of one.

Focat tailed him quietly. Focat was a lynx. Tiansu had found him during a hunt. He was only a cub then.

Focat's mother had died confronting a bear, and his mother had passed away from an ague, a rare illness that not even the shaman could treat.

Tiansu's brother had been one of the Khan's best cavalrymen. He was not partial to Tiansu keeping Focat, citing that it was dangerous to have a meat-eater in the tribe. Unless, of course, Tiansu wanted a nice fur vest.

That was the first time that Tiansu had opposed his brother; then he fed Focat using pieces of horse meat and threads of mutton.

Another day with the shamaness, Tiansu thought as he went out of his yurt.

Uncle Dazhe stood near, patting away dew on his legs.

They greeted each other and chattered while walking towards the night guard.

"Has the shamaness done anything out of order?"

"Still the same," Tiansu replied. "No spells cast, nothing suspicious."

"Our Khan has been devising a most important move. Keep a close eye on her; we cannot let her stymie his master plan."

"Yes." Tiansu looked back. Focat followed him still.

Many bruits had revolved around the shamaness recently.

Some said that she could heal wounds with a flick of her fingers; some said that she knew how to dish out invocations like an archer; others said that she knew the configurations of stars as if they were pastures on the Khan's map and magic spells on the shaman's grimoire, and some others said that she could predict the amount of wool and the number of flies on any sheep or horse under the sky.

But how had the shamaness arrived at their tribe?

No one knew.

Some said that she came from the welkin; others said she was a spy sent by their nemesis, the Northern Wei; still others said that the Tengri had appointed the shamaness so she could aid their Khan because her pelisse resembled the colour of the fiercest sun.

Tiansu did not know whom to believe. On the day of the tribal ritual, he went to pick herbs. According to Uncle Dazhe, the shamaness had arrived on a beast. The beast had looked like a white fox but was as large as a horse, with a long, white tail. No one had ever seen such a creature before.

Tiansu walked into the pen, and the sheep welcomed him. Perhaps they could sense that they were moving to another pasture.

Focat leapt onto a fat ruminating sheep. The sheep baaed, as usual, already used to Focat's presence.

"Hey! Dazhe! Why don't you bring me more frozen sheep dung balls?!" the officer in charge of keeping attendance shouted from a distance.

"I will fetch you some now!" Uncle Dazhe shouted back. He looked at Tiansu with a stern face. "Off you go now and remember to avoid her eyes."

Tiansu nodded solemnly.

He summoned Focat, and they made their way to the tent where they kept the mysterious shamaness.

The day dawned.

Tiansu spoke with the night guard, asking if anything was out of order yesternight. The other party shook his head as he yawned.

Tiansu went into the yurt and saw the shamaness leaning against a stack of hay, carving on a piece of wood using a blunt stone. He settled on the sheepskin laid on the ground. A few sowbugs crawled by his feet.

Focat stood beside Tiansu's right knee and licked his paws with a satisfying purr.

Sometimes, Tiansu would envy Focat's composure, especially in moments like this. He sensed that the shamaness was staring at him. Then she let out a sigh.

The wood cage offered Tiansu the chance to observe the shamaness without her knowing. Through the thorny bars, he saw the beast that accompanied her.

It was a small animal, even smaller than Focat, with a white mane.

How rumours travel... There was no way to mistake a fox for a horse, Tiansu thought as he disconnected his scabbard from his weapon belt and stropped his knife with a corner of the sheepskin.

"Feee..." The little beast walked up to the wooden fence and called out.

Focat approached the cage cautiously, keeping his distance.

***

It's the third day already...

Moli looked at the marks on the wood in her hand, lost in thought.

It was not a dream. Nor a movie.

She threw away the wood and checked her wrist, both of her wrists; there were no three black lines like in the movie *Jumanji*.

Not Jumanji. Not a game. Not even Pac-Man.

Moli still had only one life.

She had thought of Maggie, of her grandparents, of Aunt Edith, of her uncle, of the Big Whale sister, of Catherine and Chance, of the person who said 'tofu' on the aeroplane, and even Miss Warner, her English teacher.

Moli feared that she would never see them again.

Only knowing to cherish when you lost them...

She suppressed her tears once more. However, it was getting more difficult to do so.

"Fiiiiii~"

Moli looked at the animal beside her; her companion in this wood cage and the foreign world. She called it Feifei.

Moli had read from *The Classic of Mountains and Seas* about a mythical creature called Feifei – a fox with a mane and a long, white tail. The book also said that Feifeis are renowned for alleviating people of their sorrows.

Moli couldn't quite remember what happened when she fell from the universe, but she knew that it was Feifei who saved her. Her thoughts drifted once again to Qiuniu's *guqin*, and the other sons of the dragon, and Xuanwu's question.

Moli checked the wound on her palm; it had scabbed with a grainy surface.

When she was captured and taken into this hut, Moli had found some wet tissues in her pocket to clean the wound, probably put in there by her mother.

A time slip...

Moli did not know if she had had a time slip. Something was unsettling about the phrase that gave her a sense of surrealness. What happened to the original world? Her world?

Moli reached her left hand into her coat pocket. There were a few other wet tissues, a small USB that was once a cloud, a candy, and a lip balm. There had been a mask as well.

On the first day she'd been locked in, Moli had remembered a book that her teacher had recommended: *Guns, Germs, and Steel*, a history book detailing how the Europeans brought guns and germs to the New World. While many of the indigenous populations died from wars, many more had died from measles and smallpox.

The pandemic!

Moli dared not to think further and quickly threw her mask into the fire.

"Feeeiiii~" Feifei called out at her feet.

Moli crouched down and pretended to sleep, but she quietly observed the guard in charge of watching her.

She had tried to escape the cage, and it didn't work.

There were two guards: an older one for the night, who slept through the night, and a younger one who was alert at all times. He had a lynx with him.

Moli had found that the young guard always liked to clean his dirk. She didn't know if he did it on purpose or not.

Moli felt a stab of pain in her mouth. She had a bad ulcer there. She hadn't had many vegetables in the last three days. The diet of the people there was rather meat-based. However, she had offerings of milk occasionally.

Not cow's milk. Maybe goat's, Moli thought as she licked her ulcer. The pain was real.

Many of the people that she saw had clothing of fur and sheepskin, with some weaving. It was cold during night-time, and Moli tried to stay close to the fire even though she had her coat and jumper.

She tried to recall what she had read from the exhibition room at the British Museum. Might she have time slipped to Rouran?

Well, at least it beats the Jurassic. Moli laughed and sighed. She had tried many times to communicate with her guards, but to no avail.

Perhaps all those authors who have written about time travel have never experienced a time slip.

Moli could not help but make fun of the situation.

A large dung beetle rolled a dung ball past some embers in a corner of the wooden cage.

Her uncle had once told her that dung beetles could navigate using the band of light from the Milky Way to find their way home. Moli touched what remained of the digital cloud. If she could recharge it, perhaps she could find her way back to the door. Moli wondered if Xuanwu still roamed in that Corridor of War, waiting to hear if P equals NP or not.

She let out a frustrated sigh.

Her nails were still growing.

Maybe she would never go back.

No! Keep your spirits up! Never lose hope!

Moli hugged Feifei and began to hum a song. One of her favourites.

Feifei nuzzled her neck, its warm breaths a little ticklish.

Don't cry, Moli. You are a strong girl. Her grandma's words resounded in her ears.

But Moli was tired of being strong.

***

Tiansu stood up the moment the shamaness began to cast a spell.

A spell that he had never heard before.

Perhaps only the best shamans could understand, Tiansu thought as he got into a fighting posture while observing his target.

He remembered Uncle Dazhe's instructions. *"Never look into her eyes."*

The incomprehensible chanting stopped, then resumed after a while. This time the shamaness had a shakier voice.

Focat leaned into the cage, his pointed ears rotating, attending.

Could it be, Tiansu wondered, *could it be that the shamaness was crying?*

He listened for a moment longer.

Might it be a trap to divert his attention?

He was not sure.

Tiansu looked tentatively into the cage.

Then...he found himself looking directly into the shamaness' eyes.

They were as gentle as the night sky.

No!

Tiansu panicked.

He had looked into her eyes!

What would happen?

Was he possessed now?

Would he turn into a stone?

Would he turn into an animal?

Would his bones melt like spring snow?

Would his hair fall out like dead leaves?

Would his teeth weaken like gristle?

Would his stomach explode like a sheep that ate poison ivy?

Would his skin be as rough as sand?

NOOOOO!

Tiansu felt the world spin around him.

Why didn't they blindfold her!

He gave up all hope. He only wished that Uncle Dazhe would take care of Focat. And that he had no need for a fur vest.

If I see your mother again, Focat, I will tell her that you have grown into a strong lynx. I will tell her that my brother killed that bear and avenged you.

Tiansu was ready.

He was ready to die.

And then nothing happened.

Tiansu waited a while longer.

Still, nothing happened.

He waved his hands, moved his legs, pursed his lips, and took a few deep breaths.

Nothing happened.

Tiansu opened his eyes, finding Focat licking his front paws by his feet.

Ha!

He laughed at himself.

It seems the shamaness had no power whatsoever.

Tiansu looked at the girl again. She was sitting down with the beast in her arms.

That's right, he thought, *if you have any sense, you had better not meddle with our Khan's affairs.*

Tiansu wondered how the tribe of Gaoche would receive them. Would they greet them with meat and wine? Or would they oppose them with their weapons and high carts? And who would guard the shamaness when they followed their Khan to the next pasture?

Tiansu thought for a while. He would offer himself for the post.

Tiansu had heard his brother once say that the Northern Weis had a most wondrous method of hedging sheep in the night.

"First, you will need some large, sturdy tree trunks as the palisades. Circle them to make a pen, add water after nightfall, and when the water freezes, it will become a jail of ice."

Might be handy, Tiansu thought.

He saw the witch stand up and move her lips. She shouted:

"RU! RU! RU!"

Aha!

Tiansu drew his dagger as Focat arched his back and snarled.

"How dare you!" He waved his knife. "How dare you say such a forbidden word in our tribe!"

"Fiiiiiii!" The little beast began to scream as well.

Then the witch stopped shouting.

Tiansu was now confident that the witch was a spy sent by the Northern Wei.

His brother once mentioned that the Weis had devised all sorts of derogatory terms to belittle their tribe. Among them, the word *ruru* was the nastiest. It meant a 'life form as low as a worm'.

Huh! If the Northern Weis had thought the Rourans as low as worms, then they would learn their lesson the hard way, Tiansu thought.

He vowed that as long as he drew breath, he would never allow that word to be uttered on the vast grasslands and boundless deserts again.

Not even once.

Not ever again on the steppe.

Not even a syllable.

***

Moli was genuinely puzzled and perplexed.

She didn't understand why the guard was so enraged by the word "ru".

Wasn't it a surname for the Rourans' descendants?

Wasn't there a Princess Ruru?

Moli was quite sure that her mother had talked about the 'the clan of Ru from Yunzhong' the night before.

The night before...before here...and before now...

Moli slumped against the stack of hay, not minding the prickly feeling on her back.

An eagle shrieked in the distance.

She saw the guard slowly retreating to the door, and the lynx stopped licking its paws.

A cacophony of sounds made their way into the hut.

She could hear a stampede with sheep baaing, cows mooing, horses rattling, people yelling, and footsteps trampling.

It seemed as though a big shot was coming.

"That's right. Get your boss here." Moli raised her chin and told the guard.

The guard ignored her and pulled up the curtains at the hut's opening.

Then.

An eagle fluttered in.

No...not an eagle. Moli's eyes opened wide.

It was a...

It was a lidded ritual wine container in the form of a bird.

What a name to remember...

Moli had seen it once in a documentary, about a bronze wine container made by a craftsman during the Spring and Autumn

Period in Chinese history. Zizha, the craftsman, loved birds and had created many bird-formed bronze objects.

The wine container was shaped like an owl, and was about twenty-five centimetres tall and twenty centimetres wide. It had a streamlined body with eyes decorated with yellow onyx. Its head, feet, and beak were forged separately and joined by mortise and tenon. What Moli liked the most about that wine container was that it had motifs resembling dragons.

The documentary said the bird-shaped container represented the pinnacle of bronze object making in the Spring and Autumn Period and it was stored in the Freer Gallery of Art in the US.

Yet...

The very same wine container now rested on top of her cage and watched Moli intently with its glaring eyes.

Moli was speechless.

Another round of clamour.

The guard genuflected and the lynx lowered its head as if paying obeisance.

A stout man in a full-bodied tiger fur coat and an ermine fur vest walked in. He had a long scar on the left side of his face and a leather hat with a piece of solid gold in the middle.

Following him was a lanky, slovenly fellow, dressed in a black robe, holding a cane made from bones. His cane had several small bells hanging from it, and two long motley feathers ruffled and revolved on top, like an antenna. This fellow wore several pendants and a necklace made from a bear's tooth. He had a beard that looked like curled headphone cords.

Then...Moli was left speechless once again.

Two small beasts entered. One was the colour of lavender, the size of a bulldog, and had spikes on its back. The other had a body like a small rhinoceros, green fur, and the head of an ox. Weren't they the very same stone beasts that Moli had seen at the Rouran exhibition?

"Bei, bei, bei," the purple beast said.

"Par, par, par," the green beast noised.

Only after the two beasts entered the hut did the young guard and the lynx straighten their posture.

Moli watched the bronze bird as it whirred its wings again and landed on the shoulders of the large man. Then the thin, black-robed man waved his cane, and the two beasts went quiet.

Moli took Feifei into her arms, stood up, and faced them. She could hear the sounds of mechanical gears, like the old clock in Grandma Hua's house.

What might be its innards?

Moli listened as the bronze bird made the sounds.

She wondered if the bronze bird also made use of digital energy.

If only the Rourans had computers, Moli thought, touching the USB in her coat pocket.

Chapter 8

"Anything unusual about the shamaness?" the shaman slurred.

"She did attempt to incant, but nothing happened," Tiansu replied reverently.

Focat neared him. Tiansu knew that he was not very fond of the shaman's companion beasts.

"My most esteemed Khan," the shaman cleared his throat, "a few days ago I sensed that the Tengri would send a shamaness to assist with our cause. Now that she is here, it ought to be a most promising sign for our meeting with the Gaoches."

"As you say, my shaman, should we find a more comfortable tent for our divine guest? And bring her the finest food and some horse milk wine, perhaps?"

The shaman knew that the one good way of destroying a person was through flattery. He had cajoled the Khan into being his puppet a long time ago.

"No one is as wise as you, my Khan," the shaman said, stroking his beard, "and we must have the most capable warriors to protect her."

Tiansu hesitated; he did not know if he should volunteer for that post or not.

"And," the shaman continued with his turbid voice, "our dearest guest would need a suitable outfit so she can perform her magic. I will endeavour to call for a set of silver armour from the sky."

"Kke! Eke!" the bronze eagle, the Miragle, barked on the Khan's shoulder.

"What's wrong, old chap?" The Khan looked sideways. "Would you like some nosh?"

The Miragle cawed twice for yes.

Tiansu nodded to the Khan and left the tent.

"Can it be true that the shamaness can heal wounds with her hands?" Khan petted his Miragle while asking. "Us Rourans would no doubt prosper, now aided by her power."

"Our most esteemed Khan!" someone shouted outside and scurried into the room. "The patrol team had sightings of a chariot falling from the sky!"

"Oh?" The Khan frowned. "Shaman, what an unusual happening."

"My bravest Khan, who is known far and wide, please rest assured." The shaman gave a sly smile. "Last night, when I gazed at the stars, I had also learnt that the Tengri would send us a chariot to aid your expedition. It would be a most valuable asset for us. That chariot alone would defeat a thousand carts of the Gaoches."

"If the Tengri shall choose to grace me with this power," the Khan let out a breath, "I will go and inspect that chariot now."

He paused. "How about if I leave my Miragle here to assist your cloud calling?"

"That would be most kind of you, my most considerate Khan."

The Khan raised his arm slightly, and the Miragle flew up on the top of the wood cage once again. "I will be back in half a shake of a lamb's tail. Your food shall be here soon."

Before leaving, the Khan had accidentally stepped on the purple beast's tail, but he failed to notice.

Damn it! The shaman cursed inwardly. *You brute! You've hurt my baby pet!*

He looked up to the metal bird and reminded himself to calm down.

That duffer still didn't trust me enough, so he made that bird spy on me… but wise as an ass may be, it can never outsmart a groom.

The shaman took a deep breath.

Patience. Patience is a virtue.

After all, he had waited for years, even decades, for the Rourans' demise.

A few more days was no big deal.

No one knew, but the shaman himself, that he was a Gaoche undercover. His mission had started when he was still a child. One day, his tribe's leader had saved an elder. The elder had a face with wrinkles like a dried riverbed, fingers like blades, limbs like stakes, and a tongue armed with teeth.

The wizened elder showed his appreciation by spending a night learning the sky. Then he divined with fifty stalks of dry grass. He had told their leader that the Gaoches would perish in the hands of the Rourans, and if they wished to gain the upper hand, they must plan ahead.

"Ekha!" the metal bird squawked.

Wait till your master crawls under my feet and begs me to end his life! Then I will pull out your beak and make you a bowl for my pets! the shaman execrated.

His plans had worked perfectly well. Except...

At first, there was the witch. Now a chariot. The elder had mentioned neither.

He observed the caged girl. Although she was dressed oddly, she had only an ordinary appearance.

Not enough to cause problems. But...

He shot a baleful glance in the direction of the small, white beast resting in the cage. He sensed that it was no ordinary beast.

Perhaps I could take care of it now. Only if the bird was not looking...

His companion beasts had sensed his upset. They shifted restlessly.

Could he allow this chance to pass?

The shaman smiled.

Better do it before Tiansu comes back.

Moli stood there, jaded.

She now understood what it was like to be an animal in a zoo, feeling the gaze and leers of others all the time. She was exhausted.

She crouched down once again, leaning against the haystack, and hugged Feifei.

She could not give up yet.

She still needed to teach Aunt Edith a new Chinese word every day.

She still needed to tell Grandma Hua about the exhibition.

She still needed to figure out if P equalled NP or not.

She still had so many things to do.

"Yay!" the bronze bird squeaked again.

Moli opened her eyes and saw the young guard was back. He held a rough stone bowl with some dark liquid. A few drops ran down the edge and fell to the ground.

The lynx licked at them.

The bronze bird perched on the young guard's arm and began to drink from the bowl. A rotten smell permeated the hut.

The skinny man stepped aside and covered his nose, his two beasts following him.

Moli sniffed hard. She thought she had smelled blood.

Animal blood.

The bronze bird gulped the contents of the bowl. Later, charcoal smoke emerged from its beak.

Moli watched as the smoke belched out like a steam train.

A bronze bird powered by blood...

A miniature Stegosaurus with a snout of a pig...

A white fox with a horse's mane...

A tank-sized tortoise...

A serpent who speaks...

Moli felt that she now had an extensive collection of mythical creatures in the library in her head.

***

The Miragle gave a contented sigh and rubbed its beak against Tiansu's chest.

Tiansu placed the stone bowl on the ground. Focat couldn't wait to lick it.

"Tiansu, why don't you bring the shamaness to the Tree of Life while I go and prepare?" the shaman said with a muddy voice. "And clean up her filth. Even vultures could not enjoy the stench in this squalid tent."

"Yes, my shaman."

The shaman left and waved his trident made from deer's bones. His two companion beasts followed.

As the purple beast liked to make 'bei' sounds and the green beast 'par' sounds, Tiansu had named them Beipar and Parbei. He had heard that people gave dogs these names in tribes in the West.

Focat had licked the stone bowl clean.

Tiansu bent down and retrieved the bowl. The Miragle waited for him to open the curtains and then flew out of the tent.

He untangled the enmeshed leather ropes that served as a lock to the cage, took out his knife, and walked into the cage.

"Feeei," the small, white beast voiced as it ran to Focat.

"Watch out!" Tiansu turned and warned Focat.

The two animals stood still, then quickly gambolled around like two cubs.

The shamaness looked at him, but Tiansu still avoided her eyes.

"Follow me," he told her as he gestured.

Fine, Moli thought. She could do with some fresh air.

Moli made her way out of the cage, her legs a little unsteady and numb.

When she went out of the hut, she realised that she had been kept in a yurt.

Moli recalled the story she had read at the exhibition, about a shamaness who had kidnapped the Khan's younger brother and ordered the Khan to build a large tent.

Maybe...maybe they mistook me for a shamaness?

"Eke!"

Moli looked up and saw the bronze bird hovering above, then headed towards the east.

The sun was the same.

At least she hoped it was.

But the world was no longer her world.

The guard kept a wary eye on Moli, probably fearing she might escape.

Moli found him to be a few years older than her.

The guard grabbed a corner of Moli's coat and tugged on it, so Moli followed him in the direction the bronze bird had flown.

There were yurts, rows of decrepit tents.

Some people carried jars of milk, and others leather whips; some sewed garments with bone needles; others counted sheep dung balls. Some smoked meat over cinders, others skinned their game; some dried herbs and caul, others shaped stones.

Some sang and some danced.

All of them stared at Moli.

If only Morris was here.

She kept her gait even, not long before seeing a large rootless tree covered with rime that floated in the air.

***

Tiansu wiped the beads of sweat from his forehead and turned. In the distance, Focat and the little beast chased each other and scampered.

"Eiih!" The Miragle landed on his shoulder, its claws a little too sharp for comfort.

"Bring forth the shamaness to the Tree of Life!" the shaman ordered.

Beipar the purple beast and Parbei the green beast stood beside him.

"Yes!" Tiansu replied loudly.

He led the shamaness to the Tree of Life, gestured to her not to move, then tied her onto the tree with leather ropes the way he would tie up a sheep.

The shamaness' companion beast rushed to her feet and whined incessantly.

"Now, step back," the shaman ordered again as he held the sacred drum. The bells garnishing his waist jangled.

"Focat, follow me now." Tiansu waved at Focat, who seemed a little reluctant to leave the white fox. When Focat failed to respond to his instructions, Tiansu walked over and picked him up.

Focat was heavy, as heavy as two newborn lambs.

Perhaps I have fed you too well, Tiansu mused.

Beipar let out a 'bei' and walked towards the shamaness, then Parbei gave a 'par' and approached her as well.

The Shaman sing-songed a short verse.

"Bei, bei, bei..."

"Par, par, par..."

Beipar and Parbei circled the tree as they ran. One followed the direction of the sun; the other followed the way of river.

Then the Shaman stopped his chanting, raised his hands well above his head and up toward the sky.

Cloud calling had begun.

***

When Moli saw the thin man in the black robe again, she almost didn't recognise him.

The man wore a violet-black wooden mask with several skulls carved into his forehead. There was an extra eye between the brows, and it bulged like a rotten apple. The mask also depicted four exposed canine teeth.

He wore a strange get-up, like an exorcist in a horror movie.

There was a leather cap with a piece of shiny metal that looked like copper. Threads of the colours of the rainbow weaved together to tie onto the back of the cap. A small metal bell bounced on his back every time the man chanted.

He also wore a large dress made from multicoloured leather ribbons that resembled scarfs. Besides, he had several hangings of snakeskin around his torso.

A large bronze mirror decorated the middle of his chest, and smaller, round mirrors the size of CDs hung on his shoulders and arms. He had a belt made from leather and various animal bones and teeth, and pointy shoes with mirrors on them as well.

He looked resplendent.

Moli watched as the man stood upright, his head bobbing and his hands shaking. The man sang and spun his body a hundred and eighty-eight times.

She counted every time.

"Den~Ri~Oh~Ah~Ge~Ge"

He raised his heads as if he wanted to communicate with the immortals.

Slowly, a fallstreak hole formed in the sky.

"Ka~An~Ai~Ke~Ve"

The man spun so fast that his robe floated. As his singing and cantillating and shouting continued, anvils of clouds gathered, obscuring the sun.

Moli watched in awe as the asperitas cloud cover rose, swirled, tumbled, separated, and merged, finally forming a whirlpool.

Rain fell from the vortex like silver threads.

"Ya~ Mi~ Woo"

The man stood still and welcomed the rain and the squall. He gathered the threads as if he were weaving. The silver rain descended in a steady stream.

Moli watched in shock as the man continued to gabble.

Could it be true that every cloud did indeed have a silver lining?

Chapter 9

"Moli...Moli..."

Moli faintly heard someone calling.

A dream...

The corners of her mouth twitched.

It was a dream...

Yet, she felt something was amiss.

She was not sleep on the wooden bed at home, nor the comfy bed at the hotel, nor the haystack in that Rouran tent.

"We should only lay blame on your name, brother. 'Qiuniu', 'Qiu' meaning prisoner. Indeed! Now that we are immured..." a voice said.

"Yazi, if you hadn't borrowed trouble again, how would we have ended up here?" another voice retorted; it sounded familiar.

"If you had not spoken ill of me in front of Father, how in the universe could that gluttonous Taotie replace my position?" the first voice complained.

"For the sake of our many years of brotherly love, if you could refrain from using violence, and put a leash on your warlike nature, I could also admonish Father again..."

"Ha! How very kind of you! Now we are talking about love..." The reedy voice was full of mockery. "As I discussed with Niccolò the strategist in Florence, 'Tis better to be feared than loved'. Throughout history, there is still only Mengde Cao who understood me. He said that I 'would rather betray others than have them betraying me'. How can brothers base their connections on love and not trust? Today you let Father take my throne, and tomorrow you can let Pixiu overtake Chaofeng. What well-calculated moves. Or should I say, what wonderfully composed tunes?"

"Yazi, you... Forget it. My *guqin* is a lost cause now, and I wish to reprove you no more. One final piece of advice: you had better conduct yourself before everything is too late."

"Is that so? You can call me belligerent and combative, but I cannot even bring up that it was *you* who breached the laws and allowed a human trespasser into the Corridor of War?"

"My two most respectable elder brothers, prithee...please stop this arguing and let us not forget Father's teachings on peace and harmony," a cultured voice pleaded. "I still recall the time when we went to Florence. We had such a lovely time, each helping with our skills. Qiuniu chatting with da Vinci on the newest designs of musical instruments. Yazi discussing politics and governance with that strategist Machiavelli. And our youngest brother helping to solve the flooding problems in the Arno. Why are we quarrelling and blaming each other now? To maintain history, we need to work together."

Da Vinci...strategy...Yazi...

Why do these terms sound so familiar? Moli thought in her dream. Then she remembered.

Moli snapped open her eyes. It was pitch dark wherever she was.

A whining sough came. It sounded like singing sand.

Moli got up and felt around. Her fingers touched a garment. A little prickly. Not a garment, but...soft armour.

She remembered how that skinny black-robed man had summoned cloud and silver rain from the sky. Then Moli found a length of leather cord on her right wrist. She followed the rope... and then....

A hand!

Moli touched the hand. It was warm.

Light snoring came.

Probably the young guard...

Moli touched around and found something furry. A tail. Not as long as Feifei's.

Perhaps the lynx...

"Moli, I am sorry to have disturbed your sleep," a voice said.

"Qiuniu? Where are you? Light up your tail so I can see you."

"Huh! Light up! We can't even move in this inclement bale!" a grumpy voice said.

"Human child, my name is Fuxi, and I am the eighth son of the dragon," the genteel voice resounded. "My eldest brother Qiuniu had invited you to the Hall of Ten Thousand Sages, with unforeseen circumstances. It is with our deepest regret that you are stranded here. Our father had sent us to help you and to counteract the distortion of history." The voice paused. "Father did not wish for us to abuse our power, so he sent us here on a chariot: a stone pillar for each of us, and a stone beast at each corner."

Moli followed the voice and found herself touching a rough slab.

"Feeei!" Feifei came up, its mane glowing.

Moli saw some Chinese knots, an auspicious symbol, and propitious clouds carved on the stone along with lotus, bats, magpies, deer, gourds, peacocks, snakes, carps, phoenixes, dragons, and strands of beads and pearls.

She lifted Feifei and looked around. The chariot indeed had four stone pillars. The front left was Qiuniu.

It was the very pillar she had seen at the Rouran exhibition. *So that's it,* Moli mulled.

"Feeiii~" Feifei seemed excited to see its owner.

Qiuniu sighed softly. "I am glad that you still kept the string fairy."

Moli held up Feifei and ventured to the back of the chariot. The pillar on the left did not respond. She looked at the stone beast; it had the face of a giant lizard, with a goatee. Moli thought it must be the dragon's third son, Chaofeng.

Chaofeng was the one who liked to ascend, so people put its image on eaves of palaces.

Moli walked to the right-back pillar. The stone beast there had a dragon's head. It must be Fuxi, who loved literature and calligraphy.

She went around the chariot and found the last pillar. There was a fierce beast on it. Its teeth were bared and its eyes glared at Moli.

This must be Yazi, the one who liked wars and conflicts, so people put its image on the handles of weapons.

Moli shivered and Feifei's hackles rose.

"You little rug rat! Why would you be so scared about a mere Xuanwu? Don't you know that the best defence is attack? If they asked you questions and pressed you for answers, why didn't you ask them back?" Yazi sounded very impatient. "Why don't you ask how dark matter is distributed in galaxies? How do you verify verity and how do you defy rarity? Or at what velocity Alice has to dash to escape Wonderland?"

"Oh!" Moli was bemused. "But why would Alice want to escape Wonderland?"

"Because that Carroll stinker is a–"

"My dearest brother," Fuxi called out, "please do not unsettle the human child any further. Now that we are here, let us combine efforts and overcome this hurdle. As the old saying goes, 'it is never too late to mend a broken sheep pen'."

"Talk is cheap, my bruvver. It serves only each and everyone's own agenda. What did you contribute when we helped Leonardo and Niccolò? Did you not idle your time away with that Dante's nursery rhymes? Indeed, now that we are here, why don't you take this opportunity and produce a literary masterpiece with your gift of tongues? Umm... Here is an apt working title for it: how does *Rouran Diary: Epistles from a Lost Dynasty* sound? Umm? Lest to prove your trip was not in vain." Yazi spoke contemptuously.

"Oh! My brother! Now that...now that we are pinioned on this chariot of the dragon and unable to see beyond this tent – not to mention that I hardly know the current situation – how can I dare to make such acts of deception?" Fuxi balked at the idea.

"How hard can it be?" Yazi chortled. "*Trahison des clercs* is nothing novel. Many inkslingers have done so before, and many more will do so after. Just let your imagination run wild. You could say, 'a groom friend informed me of the barbarian nature of the Rourans, who dumped thousands of bodies in a pit'. Or, you could also jot down, 'a little bird told me that there were thousands of unclaimed weapons left behind on the battlefields. And their owners have long crumbled to running sand. Such remorse for so many Northern Wei families. So much smelted metal gone to waste'. You might even add a nice illustratio—"

Qiuniu stepped in. "Yazi, you have talked entirely too much for tonight."

"A thousand cups of wine is still not enough when true friends meet, but half a sentence is too much when there is no meeting of minds." Yazi laughed coldly. "Why don't I follow Chaofeng's suit and meditate?"

Qiuniu sighed again. "Moli, I have been remiss in my duties. I should have taken you home."

"It's not your fault," Moli said understandingly. "I wish I'd been able to answer Xuanwu's question." She recalled that night. "And...I might have opened a door marked with a letter 'i'."

"You do not need to distress yourself with that." Qiuniu paused. "The enchantment mechanisms behind that door were not infringed." Qiuniu added, "I did talk to Xuanwu, and they agreed not to pursue this matter further."

Moli let out a long breath and faltered, "If...if...I hadn't escaped, what would have happened?" She recalled the tortoise stumping and the serpent hissing.

"Well, the worst would have been for you to sit through a lengthy lecture on advanced mathematics, although they might also deliver on topics of quantum computing," Qiuniu mused.

"They do love teaching. They always try to inculcate in their pupils an attitude of enquiry and a liking for mathematics."

"Oh, okay," Moli replied, distracted.

How would it feel to have Xuanwu as your Maths teacher?

She put away the thought for later.

Moli hopped on the stone chariot. The young guard still slept soundly.

She lowered her voice. "How are your brothers?"

"Thank you for your concern," Qiuniu offered sincerely. "Father ordered Pulao to the sea to enhance endurance. Bi'an had only minor injuries and is now recuperating on Kunlun Mountain."

Moli had seen pictures of that mountain range; it had beautiful clouds.

"And...the digital cloud." Moli took out the USB from her pocket. "It's here."

"We can recharge it once we return to the realm of π," Fuxi said. "Human child, our priority now is to help you and to remove any distortions of history. This will be the most delicate part, as we do not yet know what would happen because of your arrival. If this segment of history changes, it is possible to alter future events as well."

Moli bit her lips and thought.

Maybe...Maybe Morris would not die. Or he would never meet Maggie. Or Grandpa was never adopted. Or a dragon would never fall at Yingkou. Or the Summer Palace was never destroyed. Or the indigenous people of the New World never died of germs...or guns...

"Humans make history; we only remember," Qiuniu reminded her. "Altering the path of history runs the risk of a world reboot. Those who attacked us at the Hall of Ten Thousand Sages were the very same who wanted to roll back your world to *Tianyuan*, the nexus of the Universe, to its original state."

A reboot, Moli muttered to herself. Her grandma had always told her grandpa that whenever there was something wrong with the computer, he should reboot it.

But sometimes rebooting didn't work.

"Perhaps I am the one who has been talking too much tonight." Qiuniu sighed again. "It's quite late. Please get some more sleep."

"But how will we know if history has changed?" Moli asked.

"The moment the path of history alters, the Chinese knots engraved on this slab will glow. And they will cease to do so when we correct the course of history again."

Moli nodded as she touched the pitted areas. A week ago, she thought that she had understood how most things worked. Now she was not that sure anymore.

Moli curled up beside Feifei and pondered.

The magazine article had said that most anecdotes about the Rourans were found in historical texts by the Northern Wei. Might it be that historians would undergo a time-slip rather than getting all their information from only a few one-sided books?

Moli's uncle had read many diaries and watched many vlogs of people who had lived in Wuhan during the lockdown. There were accounts of volunteers, taxi drivers, foreigners, teachers, and medical staff who went to provide support.

Her uncle said, "There is a fine line between fiction and non-fiction, and between compilation and fabrication."

Moli sat up on this note. "Qiuniu," she asked, "is there any way I can understand the Rourans' language?"

After a while, Qiuniu responded: "There is only one way."

***

In the morning, Tiansu rose early to prepare and untether the horses. They reared as Uncle Dazhe walked over, carrying his whip.

"This is a ton of a chariot," he said as he felt the massive stone slab. "Why would the shaman leave us with this impediment?"

Tiansu leaned against a roan horse's flank and his height had yet to reach its withers. "Our shaman said that this is a sky-sent chariot for the shamaness. It alone could fend off a thousand carts of the Gaoche."

"We should never take our enemies lightly," Uncle Dazhe said with a stern face. "You have never seen the Gaoches' high carts. The wheels are as large as domes. Their cavalries are strong and unyielding. We shall always reconnoitre."

"Yes," Tiansu agreed, "but we are no palfreys either." He tightened the lariat.

Uncle Dazhe got into his seat and ordered, "On the count of three: One! Two! Three!"

The horses rattled, and the chariot gave way only an inch.

"Once more!" Uncle Dazhe thrashed while Tiansu pushed.

The chariot finally trundled.

Tiansu got onto the chariot and touched the mysterious figures carved on the stone, wondering what it meant.

Focat sat in a corner, sulking. Tiansu then remembered that he had not seen the small fox beast since the first light. The shamaness was still asleep on the chariot. Out of caution, Tiansu tied the leather rope on her hand to a stone pillar.

He almost thought that he had seen the animal on the pillar moving, then laughed it off.

Sometime later, the shamaness woke and sat up.

Tiansu saw her lips move.

"Untie me, please," she said.

Wow, Tiansu marvelled. *Our shaman was indeed the most powerful. As soon as he called for clouds, the shamaness could talk.*

He hesitated for a while, then said, "Do not attempt to run."

He untied the rope only when she agreed.

Tiansu borrowed a horse from an elder, connected his scabbard to his weapon belt, and made his way to the leading Khan and shaman, for they had ordered him to notify them of any anomaly forthwith.

"Yey!" He heard Khan's Miragle howl.

"Giddy-up!" Tiansu spurred and galloped across the arcuate sweep of dunes.

He could see them now. The shaman rode on his piebald, one-humped camel, conversing with the Khan, who was ensconced on his war bear.

On each side of the camel drooped a sack made from caragana with Beipar and Parbei inside.

"My most powerful shaman!" Tiansu geed up the horse and came to the fore.

The shaman turned reluctantly. "Is anything the matt'r?"

"After yesterday's cloud calling, the shamaness now speaks like us." Tiansu slowed his horse to a trot.

"Just as I expected." The shaman raised his chin and looked down his nose. "Go at once and tell her to wear my silver cloud armour. Then her power will multiply towards the sky."

"Yes, our most formidable shaman. I will do so at once." Tiansu received his instructions willingly as he turned the horse.

"My dear friend and most prominent shaman, thank you for having equipped our warriors with the Tengri's silver cloud armour," the Khan said as he shifted on his bear. "Could you enlighten me on how exactly the shamaness will help us with our meeting with the Gaoches?"

"Oh, my Khan, whose name is feared in these boundless deserts, last night I sacrificed sleep to watch the sky. If the Gaoches were so hare-brained as to think that they could assail us, we are most fortunate to have the aid of the shamaness, whose power will grant us the most valuable defence. The mighty shamaness will provide us with group protection and our herd's immunity. Even the strongest arrow and the fiercest dagger could not hurt us. Her mere presence behoofs us all." The shaman stroked his scraggly beard as if tending to a bonsai. "I would suggest you, my most powerful Khan, pass on a message to the squad leaders with your most exquisite Miragle, that no soldier of ours should attack until the shamaness commands them to do so, lest her magic goes phut."

The Khan was bewildered. "But...But what if the Gaoches charge at us? We cannot even attack? Of course, I value your input, my shaman, but it does sound awfully like letting the enemy scythe through our troops until they stop because there's no one left to kill."

"Rest assured, my bravest Khan, who concerns for his people," the shaman confirmed with a toothy grin, "how can a mantis stop a chariot? Our triumph is foreordained, and all their efforts will be bootless. We are favoured by divine intervention in sooth. Any Gaoche attack will be as feeble as any attempt to make fire with water."

"Well... If you insist." The Khan whistled for the Miragle. Ten or so seconds passed and it landed on his shoulder. He caressed his pet with his fingers. "Tell my squad leaders that if the Gaoches assault, they should refrain from attacking and wait for the shamaness to lead our charge."

He finished speaking and knocked twice on the beak of the Miragle.

A mechanical voice repeated, "If the Gaoches assault, refrain from attacking and wait for the shamaness to lead our charge."

"Go and pass on my message," the Khan instructed, and the Miragle glided away.

"Thank you, my Khan, for allowing me to lead on, and what a curio of a bird you have!" the shaman commented as he watched the bronze bird disappearing beyond the skyline.

"My father knew of a craftsman whose master came from a body of water in the West. He made this Miragle for me. We had oft spoken of the camelopards that he once seen as a child."

"Truly superb! Truly superb!" the shaman blurted out while hiding laughter.

He thought as he avoided the Khan's eyes.

Sun, shift faster. Moon, manifest quicker.

Tonight, when the moon is full, my people will cull your numbskulls.
People of Rouran, lay blame with your lame Khan.
For he was the one who made you dying and us slaying.

The shaman chuckled inwardly. He had perfected the potion that fabricated the cloud armour, a thin layer that could not even defend against a sting from a horsefly.

The shaman looked up and checked the sun's position.

Oh! My travelling lamp. Wait till we stamp.

Chapter 10

When the sun disappeared, the Khan observed the clouds on the horizon and decided that it was time for the horde to rest.

He took out an arrow from the quiver installed on his war bear's back, drew his bow, and shot the arrow.

"Whoosh!" The sharp sound cut through the sky.

The arrow had a particular design to act as a whistle so that when his people heard it, they knew it was time to set up camp and dight for the night.

The shaman shivered and rose from his slumber.

"My shaman, why don't you plant your feet onto the ground and unwind a bit?" the Khan said as he descended his war bear. "We shall camp here tonight."

"Ah. My Khan, wise as usual," the shaman praised fulsomely as the black and white camel lowered itself, and he stepped on its head and dismounted. The feathers on his deer-bone trident twirled like a caracal's ear tufts. "I had sensed a particular aura in this place that would help our cause," he said as he took notice of the faint moonlight.

Upon hearing the Khan's whistling arrow, Uncle Dazhe put away his whip. "Tiansu, let us cross that sand knoll ahead, then we shall rest."

No reply came.

He turned around and saw Tiansu, holding the lynx in his arms, chatting with the shamaness and teaching her a game using coloured knuckle-bones of sheep.

Little'uns are still just little'uns, Uncle Dazhe smiled.

Later, after a quick bite, Tiansu went and found the Khan and the shaman. They had not yet finished their meals. The war bear rested nearby with the Miragle on its back. Beipar and Parbei fought over a chunk of beef jerky by the fire.

The moon was out that night. Bright and round.

A cold breeze swept across the sands.

"The shamaness ate some meat and drank some milk, but did not have the soup," Tiansu reported.

"Take good care of our shamaness," the shaman said, turning away from the fire, hiding half of his face in the shadows of chiaroscuro. "For our meeting tomorrow with the Gaoches, the shamaness and her chariot would be most useful." He spoke through a mouthful of deer blood soup.

"Please entrust me with this responsibility." Tiansu genuflected and left.

Having sent Tiansu away, the shaman looked around at the Rourans.

Eat all you can, drink all you can; this is your last night.

He drank all of his soup, satisfied, then he felt something solid against his teeth.

He chewed it. It didn't feel right, so he spat it out.

The shaman neared the fire and looked into his hand; two stone fragments rested there.

Alas!

He felt so discomfited that he almost kicked his purple beast.

The Miragle tilted its head and stared at the shaman.

He calmed himself and thought, *perfect timing to ad-lib.*

He waved his deer-bone trident and said, exasperated, "Cook! Where is the cook?! Get here at once!"

"Your excellency, I am here at your service." A tubby figure squeezed by the crowd.

"Ye wicked cook! How dare you! How dare you put rabbit shit in my soup!" The shaman narrowed his eyes, and his beard rose in anger.

"What?" The cook defended herself. "I never have... It must be a mistake...the second cook...the second cook made a mistake–"

"Hmph! Damnation! You slow reptile! So long as we haven't yet reached the Gaoches, or else they might think that we Rourans all drink rabbit shit soup!"

The Khan was left perplexed as he watched the shaman launching a diatribe against the cook. "Please, my shaman, do not let anger fog your mind." He tried to make peace. "Our cook has shown allegiance through and through. And..." he hesitated, "you have always spoken highly of her dishes."

"Such effrontery and contumely! It gives me every reason to believe that you have collaborated with the Gaoches to conspire against us! That it was your scurrilous intention to poison our troops. We shall flog her! I shall give her a crool 'ard beating. Someone brings my horsewhip!" The shaman's face empurpled, and his two companion beasts made threatening noises.

"My dear shaman, would you show your generosity once again for my sake? I will make sure that no further lapses occur," the Khan intervened. He felt he was trying to stop children from quarrelling.

"Please, my Khan, I do not wish to offend or be at loggerheads. I am merely worried that if I were to be taken ill, no one would support you and stand by your side when we negotiate with the Gaoches tomorrow. And look at this cook; she eats like a gobbler. When our soldiers charged, she simply roistered. When they fought on the frontline, she would grab twenty-five pounds of meat for herself first! Never caring for our people like you would, my most considerate Khan!" the shaman exclaimed as he watched the ascending moon. Then, he grovelled. "Forgive me, my Khan. I feel I might have stressed myself with the upcoming meeting with the Gaoches." He rose and softened his voice. "I would very much like some time to myself for now," he said as he dragged his deer-bone trident towards a small dune, followed by the two beasts.

"Please have some rest," the Khan said, "and we shall discuss tomorrow's plan later."

Then, he offered a word or two of comfort to the cook.

No one but the Miragle saw the Shaman leaving on his black and white camel.

***

Everything happened in a blur.

The minute before, Moli had been chattering with the young guard.

He had told her his name, "Tiansu", which means to grow into a stallion.

He had also explained how the Northern Wei insulted the Rourans with the word *"ruru"*.

He had also said that the progenitors of the Northern Weis were so bloodthirsty and ruthless that whenever they enthrone a prince, they would kill his mother so that she could not interfere with the new king's governance.

Tiansu was telling her that their Khan needed to negotiate a peace treaty with the Gaoches, though he feared that the Khan's uncle, Pihouba, who had his eyes on the throne, would thwart their efforts. Then he described to Moli the dreadful high carts of the Gaoches.

High carts...

Moli remembered the red double-decker she rode with Edith only days ago.

Everything was tranquil.

A gentle zephyr, sounds of insects, the crackles of a fire...

The smell of soot, horse manure, and her sweaty hair...

Pandemonium broke out in a mere second.

Screams, cries, curses, the neighing of horses, the tearing of tents, the mewling of children...all crashed into Moli's ears.

She sensed a peculiar sweetness in the embittered air. Then she realised it was the metallic tinge of blood.

Blood had eclipsed the moonlit night.

"Shamaness! Please command us to charge!" a voice bawled over the sound of weapons slashing heads and axes chopping torsos.

"Shamaness! Now!"

Moli stood still; everything was like a stop-motion animation.

The cavalryman raised his sword breakers. A man fell off his horse, picked up a torch and hurled it into a tent. A man waved his machete, severing a horse's front leg. Whirling blades hewed off fingers.

NONONONONONONONONONONONONONONONONONO NONONONONO

Moli covered her ears, closed her eyes, and shut herself from this world.

Is this history? Is this war?

Are these screams the sounds of the Rourans?

Qiuniu had retrieved Feifei in exchange for her to talk with the Rourans.

But she wanted to listen no more. She wanted to listen to this heart-wrenching hellscape no more.

"Our mighty shamaness! I beg you to charge!" Tiansu shouted.

What to do? What to do now?

Moli was no shamaness. She was just an ordinary person who wanted to live.

"Shamaness!"

Moli opened her eyes and saw the Khan streaked across the sands on a bear.

Not a dream...

How Moli wished it was a dream. Everything was besmirched with blood.

There was blood on the bear.

There was blood on the man.

There was blood on the moon too.

Not a dream...

"Shamaness! Lead us to charge!" The Khan's frantic shouting echoed.

"Yahyahyahyahyah! This is the most infuriating camisado I have ever seen!" another voice growled.

Yazi!

Moli hopped onto the chariot. "What should I do? What... what can I do?"

Yazi glared. "Take off your silver armour so they can't tell you apart!"

"Take off the silver armour!" Moli shouted at Tiansu.

The Khan had heard her as he drew his bow and arrow. "Take off your silver armour! Attack!" There was a sharp whistle followed by more reports of weapons dinting.

"Someone protects the shaman!" the Khan ordered.

"I will go!" Uncle Dazhe said as he strangled an enemy with his riding crop. "Where is he?!"

"My powerful shaman, come and help us!" the Khan called out as he axed another attacker.

Moli heard the faint fluttering of the bronze bird's wings. She saw the bird squawk, then open its beak.

"Haha! I've been lurking in that *ruru* mishmash for more than a decade, and now I can finally bring glory to my people. Hahaha!"

The shaman's peals of laughter melted into the battlefield.

If Moli hadn't strayed into Rouran, Uncle Dazhe would have caught up with the black and white camel and brought back the heads of the shaman and his two beasts.

The Chinese knots engraved on the chariot of dragon shone with a dazzling wave. At that moment, the course of history changed.

"Witch! I will gladly accept your head and I shall scalp it before sunrise!" A horse came galloping with a man on its back brandishing a pair of sword breakers, and he aimed them at Moli.

"You shall ask me first!" Uncle Dazhe strode forward with full speed and clouted the horse with his body.

The war bear rushed up, its claws digging into the man's chest.

The night grew.

After what seemed like an eternity, the first shred of light came.

Moli stood transfixed, hoping to cry, but she couldn't.

The one lying not far away, with a slash on his back, was the night guard. The one who had lost an arm built her fire.

One...two...seventeen...

Moli dared not count. She had remembered the latest figure for COVID-19 global deaths.

People...just people...

If there was no pandemic, Moli could have become their friend, their relative, their student, their neighbour, or even just passers-by on the street...

She had lost myriad possibilities.

Everyone had lost and the world had lost.

"If humans unite, one day, they will realise the truth." Qiuniu's voice cut through her haze.

The sun came out.

Moli clambered onto the chariot and looked at the stone-carved Chinese knots that still glowed faintly.

The Khan stumbled down from his war bear, and Uncle Dazhe supported him.

The bronze bird landed on the chariot and regurgitated.

"Haha! I've been lurking in that *ruru* mishmash for more than a decade, and now I can finally bring honour to my people. Hahaha!"

"That knave! That! That—" the Khan stomped his feet and beat his chest. "That scoundrel! He bamboozled me all these years! His perfidy sickens me! All his sordid plans! I've always thought he devoted his heart only to the tribe. But now! A traitor who massacred my people! He is below a man! He is a mushroom! The Gaoches... Plundering and burning...kidnapping our children and livestock," the Khan roared. "I could accept losing if the enemy outnumbers us, or if they outfox us...But NEVER! NEVER BY DECEPTION AND MENDACITY! My soldiers! My warriors! My people! They hadn't sold their lives dearly!"

"Huh! How only is 'only'?" Yazi retorted. Its eyes glared like billiard balls; its nostrils flared. "Was it only wishful thinking, or only blind faith, or only one false step that brought everlasting grief?"

The Khan kneeled. "The divine chariot of the Tengri! I am Yujiulü Shelun the Qiudoufa Khan from Yunzhong, the sixth grandson of Yujiulü Mugulü! I beg thee! Now my tribe are in dire straits! Please aid us to avenge the wrongs done to my people! I shall sacrifice every ounce of me!"

Yunzhong... The clan of Ru from Yunzhong. Moli recalled her mother's words.

She looked at the scar-faced man in front of her. How she wanted to tell him that many, many, many years later, one of his descendants would adopt a baby who would become her grandfather...

Moli felt a strange, distant, yet heart-warming connection.

"Nero fiddled while Rome burned; and you addled. Some leaders lead, and some others putt. Commander, war is unlike geometry, and you simply cannot stare at one point, one segment, one plane," Yazi elucidated. "If you win a battle and you come home unscathed, you are a wise ruler. Yet, if you lose a fight and you remain safe and unharmed, will your men stay put?" Yazi paused. "We need to divert their resentment and ire." Its eyes clouded with concern. "Chaofeng, tell me how the Gaoches are faring now."

Chaofeng...

Moli looked at the pillar that hosted the unfazed Chaofeng. It rarely spoke last night, acting as if it was no more than a stone pillar.

"If you will allow me a moment." Chaofeng closed its eyes. "They are to celebrate...a jamboree and a feast tonight."

"The most splendid chariot of the Tengri! Is this the divination of 'clairvoyance'?" the Khan exclaimed.

"Umm...it's called spectroscopy," Chaofeng explained, "or 'wind mocking' perhaps..."

"If that is the case," Yazi suggested, "Commander, why don't you send out a message saying that you have suffered a most severe wound and need a period of isolation to heal? Somewhere quiet to get inside and pull the blinds down. If the Gaoches were to have planted rats in your troops, you could let their guards relax. And now that they are planning to celebrate tonight, we can smite them on the morrow with the lark."

"My Khan!" Tiansu came racing as his horse's hooves raised gusts of sand. His clothing was torn and his left ear cut open. "We have suffered...heavily."

"Strike back in the morn, but," the Khan rushed, "the Gaoches...and their high carts... We are so outnumbered now. Manpower and supplies. We have a dearth of both."

"Huh! You poltroons! Winning concerns morale, but also solidarity." Yazi pondered. "Are your people good at woodwork?"

"My brother," Qiuniu interrupted, "if you wish to suggest an attack in a wooden horse again, remember to check if there are any olive trees around."

"Look what has got into me!" Yazi mocked itself. "As the old saying goes, 'make use of the contours when you are fighting on a mountain; make use of the currents when you are fighting on water'. We shall make use of the dunes and quicksand." Yazi looked at Moli. "Little rug rat, although this battle did not start because of you, you have played a part in it, so, tell me, what do you think we should do?"

"We...we need...we need a...strategy." Moli never thought those words would come out of her mouth.

"Well, well. Someone once wrote that 'time and surprise are the two most vital elements in war'. If you are all on board with my stratagem," Yazi cleared its throat, "pass the word on, as I said before, and gather as much food, water, and silage as you can. And the groom, would you please step forward?"

Uncle Dazhe cautiously approached the chariot.

"Go and muster your troops. Why don't we improvise on the military justice system from the Northern Wei? A chiliad of men per battalion, and every hundred as a squad, each squad a leader. Your Khan will lead the attack."

"Most divine chariot..." Uncle Dazhe hesitated. "I understand your instructions, only that..."

"A fool may talk, but a wise man speaks. Make yourself clear with no fear of ridicule," Yazi said.

"How many is a 'chiliad' of men?"

"A group of a thousand," Yazi answered.

"The Gaoche scoundrels robbed our flocks. And it may not be easy to find sheep dung."

"Why would you need sheep dung?"

Uncle Dazhe tilted his head. "To record the number of a thousand soldiers. If we don't know the number, we won't know exactly how many casualties there were."

"That's easy." Yazi chuckled and looked at Moli. "Little rug rat, I take it that you know elementary maths? Why don't you teach the groom about counting?"

Moli nodded.

It didn't take long for her to explain to Uncle Dazhe the method of notation and how to record numbers by carving on wood.

Chapter 11

Later, Tiansu trudged through the ruins of their tents. Focat followed him.

Last night. Only last night...

His elders, peers, friends, and families were dancing around the fire...sharing from the cauldron...

Yet...

Now, what remained was only soot long gone in the howling wind.

Tiansu looked up.

A bevy of vultures circled overhead, foraging for food and carrion.

Focat scared them away.

But Tiansu knew they would eventually get their portion.

He saw the shamaness searching for food and water.

He no longer knew whom to believe.

Tiansu was afraid that the "shamaness" was just another spell cast by that evil shaman.

Our Khan trusts so easily. Tiansu wept irately over the betrayal of the shaman.

"Your ear? Is it okay?"

He heard the shamaness approaching and asking. Tiansu watched her cautiously and touched his ears. Only then did he find a tear at the base of his left ear.

He saw the shamaness retrieve something from her pelisse and tear it open.

"Here...let me help you disinfect it."

Des...yinfekte...

Tiansu repeated the word in his head. He had never heard it before.

The shamaness reached out her hand. "Don't be afraid. It won't hurt. Well...maybe a bit. But only a bit."

Afraid? Tiansu thought.

I have nowt to be afraid of, not even the Tengri.

He wondered if the Tengri indeed existed.

Tiansu hesitated and took a step forward.

The shamaness' fingers were only a horse's ear away from his face. Now a lamb's nose away. Now a rabbit's tail...

Her fingers finally touched the cut on his ear. Tiansu felt a coolness, then a piercing pain.

This evil witch! Didn't they say that her fingers could heal wounds?

A lie!

The shaman was a lie!

The silver cloud armour was a lie!

And the chariot a lie!

The witch!

Tiansu looked at her.

He wanted to believe her.

"I wish I'd brought a plaster," Moli muttered.

The wound was not deep, but rather wide.

"Aunt Edith always carried a small first-aid kit with her. Her backpack had everything," she mused as she disinfected Tiansu's tear with another wet tissue.

Tiansu did not quite understand what the shamaness meant by 'first-aid' either. He waited and said, "Uncle Dazhe has some herbs to stop bleeding. I will ask him for some later to make a poultice."

"Ah~ah~ah~" Suddenly, they heard a baby hollering.

Focat's ears twirled.

Tiansu asked him to lead the way, and they found a baby under a burnt tent. A woman clutched the cradle tightly.

Moli saw her face was serene.

She wondered what Morris had looked like when he...died.

The woman's fingers were already stiff. Tiansu had to prise them open and reach for the cradle.

He found the baby's skin burning, and her fontanelle sunken, her lips parched.

"We need water!"

"There!"

Moli looked around and rushed towards a slant wagon. Droplets of water leaked from a leather sack, but it was almost gone now.

Moli knelt, found a piece of rag, dug up the wet sand with her hands, and piled the sand on the rag.

A lizard barely escaped.

She wrapped the rag tightly, wrung her hands, and squeezed out a dozen drops of water and dripped it onto the baby's forehead. Then she dipped the wet cloth on the baby's lips.

Finally, the baby stirred, puckering up her face. She opened her mouth wide and cried again as Tiansu swaddled her and crooned a lullaby.

***

The day was almost gone.

The Khan languished on a corner in the stone chariot. His war bear was not far.

He looked at the baby. "I shall raise her like my own."

"Commander, when you suffer defeats and losses, you must learn from them," Yazi said.

"A poet once wrote that 'victory or defeat is an untimely event, and it is a man who endures shame'," Fuxi counselled. "Please do not over blame yourself."

"Humph! Another poet also said that it is better to be a centurion than a scholar."

Fuxi riposted, "If Sun Tzu's strategies were all so invincible, how did Qin Shi Huang conquer his country Qi?"

Yazi ignored Fuxi. "Commander, I might as well tell you a fable."

"I'm all ears, divine chariot," the Khan replied.

Yazi's story went like this:

One day, the Emperor of a remote country received a minister in his private chamber. The minister hurried to report on a huge beast that had savaged the megalopolis.

The Emperor was shocked. "Send my praetorian guards at once to quell the beast!"

The minister replied, "Your Majesty, the guards have escorted your mother so she can visit the West Island for the summer, and will be unlikely to return today."

The Emperor said, "Put up notices offering a reward to anyone who can subdue the beast."

The minister replied, "Your Majesty, you are most wise, but the treasury is empty."

The Emperor roared, "What is going on? Where did all the money wend?"

The minister replied, "Your Majesty, to organise the Princess' coming-of-age ball last August. We have depleted the treasury with all our disports."

The Emperor was irked. "Summon the heads of the lenders and the banks apace."

The minister baulked. "I have heard that many had cashed out and bought back their shares in various sovereign ventures. I am afraid that..."

"Why must everything work against me?!" The Emperor was infuriated. "Where did this beast come from?"

The minister relayed, "Your Majesty, the beast came from a miasma of unknown origin. It has been raising havoc in a neighbouring country. They have managed to curb the beast."

The Emperor rolled his eyes and contemned. "Huh! The 'neighbouring country'? It's no more than a shanty town! How did they defeat this beast with their peccant minds as empty as a beggar's pocket under my reign? I've got it wrong, so what? Let's not be so naive as to say the other country has been much better at handling this. I'm only surprised that the beast has been able to come back so strongly. And if they knew about the behemoth, why didn't they alert us? It must be their most foul subterfuge!"

"Your Majesty, the neighbouring country had sent many messenger pigeons betokening us since January. Your Majesty, on the other hand, had turned a deaf ear on their entreaties and has repeatedly declared, 'A trivial beast! Not worth mentioning! We have it all under control! The probability of attacking by the beast was less than being hit by an asteroid!' And the dozens of messenger pigeons that came from the neighbouring country, you fed them to your eagle. Oh, My Lord!"

The minister took several steps back. "You, You, Your Majesty..."

The Emperor turned slowly and saw the ferocious beast staring at him. As experienced in slaying as he was, he did not panic. "Get my lance!"

The minister hid behind a pillar. "My great Emperor! Have you forgotten? Your lance has been sent for repair!"

"It's not fixed yet? What took so bloody long?!"

The minister knelt. "Your Majesty, you imposed a ban on trade last year so the parts could not clear customs!" He bowed and scraped. "Your Majesty, it has occurred to me that my health will no longer permit me to support you... Perhaps it is time for me to demit and step dow—"

Not waiting for the end of the minister's sentence, the Emperor grabbed him and threw him to the beast.

Yazi's voice stopped and drifted away with the blowing sand.

"My divine chariot, what you are saying is that we should never take the enemy lightly. And never attempt to neglect one's duties as a governor," the Khan reflected.

"An incompetent person could only harm oneself, yet an incompetent leader could encumber a nation. One incompetent General could exhaust a thousand armies," Yazi commented. "A man without virtue attracts criticism, while a king without virtue brings cataclysm to his people. There are kings who would admit that they have failed and learn from their mistakes."

"Then I shall endeavour to protect my people and not let them down once again with all my nisus," the Khan vowed.

The sun had set.

The baby whined in her cradle as if knowing that tonight was going to be a night that would be penned down in history.

Moli sat on the chariot as they neared the Gaoches' encampment.

After a night of singing, dancing, drinking, and indulgence, the Gaoches were sound asleep. Not even their night guards were aware of the incoming storm.

Another victory, another slaughter. Only this time, there were fewer cries.

The morning breeze brought some yelps now and then, and on a distant dune, a tumbleweed swished as it fled.

"Two wrongs never make a right and violence only breed violence," Fuxi sighed. "When humans finally understand that it ought not be rage that envelops the earth but trellises, and it should be clear springs and not hot blood that sows the desert, everything will be on the right path then."

"Alas! What a quixotic reverie you have!" Yazi said. "From the very first day of human history, there has been war. Quarrels between families, tensions between tribes, conflicts between states, and hostility between nations, battles, reprisals, invasions, world wars. As familiar with the scrolls as you are, can you tell me a single day in this physical world when there was 'total peace'? When there was true 'world peace'? Huh! Not even a single hour, a single minute, or a single second! Humans need ideals but also pragmatism. Irenic ideals will get you little princes pining for foxes and people waving a piece of paper and shouting 'this is peace in our time'! Pragmatism will get you a Machiavellian prince." Yazi paused. "From copper to bronze to iron, from muskets to machine guns, how many times has technology improved because humans merely wanted to have better weapons, to kill faster, quicker, and more easily? War can dress up as 'peace' and 'peace' can be a puppet of war. Peace is a Sisyphean venture. The value of peace is like a discounted cash flow, but who decides the discounting factor? The formulae of peace are like a Prince Rupert's Drop; a sting in the tail brings about a total teardown. Fuxi, you said once that you wished to see Kant and Bentham debate. I'd say, put them in a boxing ring and see whose theory is punchier. Who is to say what is right or wrong? And who decides between barbarism and civilisation? They say, 'Oh! We love animals; we love plants; we love nature!' And yet they are so violent to themselves. If they could divert that attention from fauna and flora to themselves, would the world be a better place? Peace requires mutual trust, and humans are known for their inability to trust. They can't even agree on the definition of a particle yet. What shall humans ever do in their infinitely repeated game of war? Peace is hard-earned and not so easily darned. For some, locking up a gun requires no less resolution than pulling the trigger. For others, they can't wait to profit from the industry of death! I'm not pro-war; I am anti-aggression. Weapons are not just weapons; they are extensions of human malice. They are extensions of humans themselves."

Will there ever be peace? Looking at the baby's sleeping face, Moli wondered.

"I have only one zillionth hope that I might one day be able to unload my armour," Yazi concluded.

Moli heard a bating of wings and saw the Miragle. Behind it, the Khan and Uncle Dazhe were on their horses.

The sun came out, shivering.

A battle had ended, yet there was no winner. One tribe's rapture was another's rupture.

When will humans ever unite?

Moli remembered that someone had said that only with global unity and a new era of cooperation could we fight the pandemic.

"One day, the humans will realise," Qiuniu said sternly, "that only they can save themselves."

Moli watched as the Chinese knots on the stone chariot glimmered.

"My most divine chariot of the Tengri!" the Khan exclaimed as his war bear pranced. "At last! I have avenged my people!"

"But that scoundrel shaman escaped. The Gaoche leader, Beihouli, has also fled!" Uncle Dazhe shouted with bile as he wiped the imbrued blood off his dagger-axe with a piece of deerskin.

"Now that we have defeated them, he and his sons will take refuge with the Northern Wei." The Khan pondered. "After we recuperate our strength, we shall move north. But before that, all search for that evil shaman!" he ordered.

"No raids required! I am here! Here I am!" A burst of cackling, eldritch laughter swirled.

Thundering supercell storms shrouded the sky and blustery whirlwinds whipped up sand curtains around them and the chariot of dragon.

"Creeping Shelun! You blockheads attacked my people! Do you know your wrongs?!" the wind howled.

"How **DARE** you say that! You! The evilest shaman! Show yourself!"

The Khan spun and shouted along with the twirling sand walls.

"You have your reason; I had mine! Yet, the steppe has its own credos! If my blood is to be spilt today, first ask if my beasts, Quicksand and Liquid Fire, agree or not!"

The sand walls crumbled like a waterfall.

The shaman stood a mile away. On his left, the purple beast was the size of an elephant. On his right, the green beast was now the size of a hippopotamus. The spikes on the purple beast's back gushed sand while the mouth of the green beast spat lava.

The surroundings were eerily quiet.

Moli saw the shaman smiling as he raised his plumed deer-bone trident. The feathers on the bone were spinning like a gyroscope.

Suddenly, the earth quaked!

Moli grabbed onto the chariot as it sank, clutching the baby's cradle with her feet.

"Who would have thought that the shaman has practised the art of sand attack!" Fuxi called out.

Moli felt as if she sat on an adrift twig, and her bearings were lost in successive waves of sand. She struggled to reach for the cradle and held the baby aloft.

Horses neighed, the soldiers screamed, and the beasts roared.

Focat cowered on Tiansu's back as he jounced in the billowing sand waves. He barely missed being hit by a horse. The Miragle was undaunted by the wind and the rushing sand; it flew high and attacked the shaman with its sharp claws.

BOOM!

The green beast spat out a lava ball that engulfed the Miragle. The bronze bird disintegrated in the air, its carcass scattering.

"I WANT YOUR HEAD NOW!" the Khan roared.

Moli saw him on his war bear, riding on the crest of a sand wave. She had never known that a bear could run that fast.

The purple beast targeted a dozen sand bombs at the Khan. The war bear swerved and hurled him onto the shaman.

They grappled and scuffled as the sand waves quietened.

"Hold on!"

The ground still trembled as Moli tossed a leather rope to Tiansu and another to Uncle Dazhe.

Just as their hands touched the ropes, the sands slid faster and faster and covered the sky once again.

"Qiuniu, do you have a way against this sand?!" Yazi enjoined.

Moli heard Qiuniu humming a tune.

The sand waves that splashed the chariot died down like liquid mercury ceasing to levitate on a magnetic field.

Moli found another piece of rope and secured the cradle on Chaofeng's pillar. Then she rose and saw that the Khan still fought the shaman while Tiansu and Uncle Dazhe crisscrossed closer as they avoided cannons of lava and grit. A squad had made their way to the back of the purple beast and attacked it in flank. The war bear burrowed its way out of the sand and knocked the green beast over.

"Qiuniu! Let's use sand to douse fire!" Yazi shouted.

"Aim for their snouts!" Chaofeng called out as well.

Qiuniu closed its eyes, concentrated, and hummed another tune.

♪ ♪ ♪

Moli heard a symphony of rising clouds and pouring rain.

The settled sands moved again, and Qiuniu's amplified humming conjured an infinite number of musical notes. A gust of wind launched them to Quicksand and Liquid Fire.

The purple beast fell first, followed by the green one.

"We shall subdue them and bring them back to Suanni," Chaofeng said.

"Ahhhh!" The Khan tumbled down and blood seeped from under his tiger coat.

The shaman clung onto his deer-bone trident. One of its feathers rived, and he barely managed to get on his feet.

He spat out a tooth and furrowed his brow. "I shall surrender my flesh to imprecate on the *rurus*!"

Chapter 12

The shaman chanted loudly as the sky darkened.

He raised his deer-bone trident high and shouted some more as flashes of lightning rolled. The trident floated high above his head.

"Qiuniu! I have never known of this spell in any books before!" Fuxi steeled itself.

"And I have sensed something bizarre with the shaman's bowels!" Chaofeng warned from its corner on the chariot.

"That shaman might smash the pot now that it cracks! He would do anything to win!" Yazi alerted the Khan.

The Chinese knots engraved on the chariot of dragon gleamed a blinding ray.

"Now is the turning point in history!" Fuxi cried out.

A bolt of lightning drew onto the deer-bone trident. It emitted beams of purple lasers then struck down and pierced the shaman's skull.

"AAAAAAHHHHHHHHHH!"

For an instant, Moli didn't know what was happening.

She'd heard a scream, thundering, and then... Moli opened her eyes, and her knees tottered.

The shaman was nowhere to be seen. In his place was a giant sepia worm as long as a mile and as wide as the entrance to a highway tunnel.

The giant worm had its mouth open wide like an operating jet turbine. It chewed up the war bear, Quicksand, and Liquid Fire.

"Sit in a theatre to see a play of hopes and fears... While the orchestra breathes fitfully the music of the spheres... That play is the tragedy, *Man*... And the hero, the Conqueror Worm..."

It laughed.

"The...the Death Worm!" Fuxi stuttered. "I have read about it only once. Its rectum is capable of discharging lightning, and its mouth spews acids!"

Uncle Dazhe and Tiansu helped the Khan as they retreated to the chariot.

"Hahaha! Creeping Shelun! Seems that I have opened a can of worms! I shall have your wriggling, impuissant *rurus* for my breakfast!"

The Death Worm opened its mouth and guffawed. Several rings of fangs contracted and expanded, and the fangs had eyes that blinked unstopping.

"As long as I draw breath, you shall never attempt to hurt my people again!"

With a whoosh, Moli saw the Miragle's beak spark like a rocket and shoot straight into the worm's mouth. The metal beak scraped an eye on the Death Worm's fang, and only raised a puff of smoke.

"Haha! What? Even a worm will turn? Perhaps I shall leave you a moment to make your will! On second thoughts, I won't. There won't be anyone left to carry it out! You should thank me, really, or why lead the life of a worm where you only eat, drink, enjoy slatterns, and snore? So let me open your eyes and enlighten your worm's-eye view." The Death Worm pelted several gushes of purple liquid that landed around the Khan. The sand there sizzled and melted like vapour.

And at that very crucial moment, the baby began to cry!

No! Moli tried to quiet her, but it was too late.

A cloud of purple venom landed in the corner on the chariot, and the stone pillar melted and turned to yellow smoke.

"Qiuniu! I shall no longer–" Chaofeng's voice broke off.

Qiuniu closed its eyes and continued to hum, and more and more notes of sand attacked the giant worm.

The Death Worm slithered quickly, rolling its body forward and zigzagging. The sand notes seemed to be as futile as peace doves trying to stop a machine gun.

Moli picked up the baby and jumped into the carriage seat, but the horses were so frightened that their hooves flicked and their tails gashed.

The chariot only lurched.

What to do? What to do now?!

Flashes of lightning and fulgurations struck and burnt the pillars of Yazi and Fuxi.

"Qiuniu! Do whatever it takes to preserve histo–" Their voices vanished.

The baby cried on.

"Moli! I have to ask you for a favour! I can't move on this pillar! Only you can do it!" Qiuniu stopped its humming. "Run towards that worm!"

Moli thought her ears were playing a trick on her. "Run... to *that* worm?"

"Trust me! Only humans can save humans!"

Moli looked at the baby in her arms and at the giant Death Worm that approached every second.

She clenched her teeth, put the baby into her cradle, and jumped off the chariot. She ran as fast as she could and dodged the sheet lightning and purple clouds.

Moli knew that there were times to escape, but this was a time to be brave.

Globs of dark venom crashed with numerous sand notes in mid-air like paintballs.

"Shamaness!" Uncle Dazhe called out hoarsely.

If this is a dream, wake me up now!

Moli was so close to the Death Worm that she could smell its obnoxious odour of ammonia and brimstone that also irritated her eyes.

The Death Worm had rent a horse on its way; the horse's leg stuck in between its serrated fangs like a toothpick as the monster masticated noisily. The eyes in the Death Worm's mouth mocked and challenged her. "If wishes were horses, I'd eat them alive just like that one."

Not a dream... And she still had only one life.

A cloud of venom almost grazed her ear and Moli dared not think about it. A bolt of lightning barely caught her coat, and Moli dared not look back.

Her legs wavered, but her mind did not.

"I can always sort the wheat from the chaff. I know you are beneath my concerns and you are just a nobody! A shamaness? Huh? You never fooled me!" The Death Worm laughed, its fangs retracting in circles. It flicked its tail, and a cloud of tinkling sand sprayed towards Moli.

"Watch out!" In an instant, Uncle Dazhe shielded her, and the Miragle's parts shot into his chest like bullets.

"Uncle Dazhe!" Tiansu threw himself by his side.

"Moli! Run!" Qiuniu sang with a high pitch.

Moli continued.

The Death Worm rolled towards her, closer every second.

Purple venom fell from the sky like a torrential downpour. Qiuniu chanted and conjured a shield of sand around her.

Yes, she was a nobody. Yes, the world was full of nobodies. Yet, it was the nobodies that made miracles. Adding up ordinary efforts, you might get extraordinary feats.

Moli felt a sudden urge to shout.

"Feeeiiiii~"

A light!

It was Feifei!

Feifei appeared, the size of a horse, hovering in the sky, glowing with a silver light. It carried Moli towards the Death Worm, dodging globs of venom and streaks of lightning.

Then, Feifei opened its mouth as if it were nickering.

But Moli could not hear a sound.

All she could hear were the growls of the Death Worm as its body curled, twitched, twisted, shrank...

"It is...not over..." the Death Worm gasped.

In the end, only a few pieces of burnt purple deer bones remained on the stilly sand.

***

The sky had cleared.

Tiansu helped Uncle Dazhe onto the chariot. He was in his final state.

"Uncle Dazhe! Uncle Dazhe!" Moli knelt beside him and took his cold hands in hers. His face overlapped with her father Morris'.

"Please don't go!" she called out.

"Here!" Tiansu fumbled with a pouch. "Herbs to stop bleeding. I've got plenty!" He poured the yellowish powder onto his uncle's chest. The powder turned into a paste as more blood gushed out from several deep wounds.

"Do...does the...sha...maness, have...a magic po...tion?" Uncle Dazhe coughed; his face distorted in agony.

Moli's vision blurred and her hands trembled as she found a lump of candy in her coat pocket. She tore it open and carefully put it into Uncle Dazhe's mouth. No one had noticed that the digital cloud's USB fell out of her pocket, and a wisp of amethyst smoke silently melted into it.

"So... sweet..." Uncle Dazhe said. He raised his hand and patted Tiansu's shoulder. "I...I...have...heard...of...the...roots...of... sweet... grass... Try... it... for me."

"Uncle!" Tiansu cried.

"Please...teach...Tian...su...how...to...use...wood...record...ing," Uncle Dazhe said with his last breath.

The Chinese knots on the chariot of dragon lost their lustre, and history resumed its original course.

Qiuniu hummed a piteous dirge.

Only the baby did not cry.

Later.

It was late into the night.

After burying Uncle Dazhe and the deceased soldiers, the Khan took the survivors back to the place where they had camped earlier.

Upon hearing of the success of their revenge, the Rourans celebrated with a grand shindig.

Now the eating, drinking, and dancing were over, leaving dying bonfires and the quietude of the night.

"How did Feifei defeat that Death Worm?" Moli asked Qiuniu.

"The string fay made use of ultrasonic waves."

"And what will happen to Yazi, Fuxi, and Chaofeng?"

"They have arrived safely back to the realm of π."

"Good to know..." Moli hugged her knees, davering. "Isn't it...isn't it nice that you don't have to worry about life...or death."

Qiuniu wanted to say something, but in the end said nothing.

Moli thought for a while, then asked, "If *ruru* is a word meant to disparage the Rourans, why did the Rouran descendants adopt this word to become their last name?"

"Could it be that initially, they wanted to remind themselves of the shame? Might it be that after a period of assimilation, they have discovered more things in common with their 'enemies' than they expected? Or could it be that they have learnt that peace was hard-earned and required delicate maintenance as a *guqin* does?"

Qiuniu paused. "Historical accounts from the Northern Wei have often depicted the Rourans as subhuman. If that was indeed the case, then why did they fight them for so long? Moli, you said that textbooks could not include everything that matters in life. You are very right. Have you noticed the lump of gold on Shelun Khan's leather cap? Did you know it is a Byzantine gold solidus? Your world was much more connected throughout history than people think it was."

"Shamaness!" Tiansu came running with Focat. "A soldier was showing off in the yurt. I reckon it is one of your...your divine objects?"

Moli sat up. By the light of the fire, she saw the USB of the digital cloud.

"Thanks." Moli took the USB, and their fingers touched.

His hand felt so very human.

The Rourans were only human. The Gaoches were only human. And the Northern Weis were only human...

Tiansu smiled. His dry lips bled.

Moli thought of giving him her lip balm, then decided against it.

If history could never be altered, how should we move on?

"It is vain to talk about building back better," Qiuniu said. "Humans have yet to realise that they have to build forward together."

Moli sat with Tiansu; she found the wound in her palm had almost healed.

A few sand grains stuck onto the scab.

Qiuniu continued, "In a dust particle, you see microcosms. And how many beings concern a human heart? Looking at the

Earth from afar, you will realize it is too small for conflict and just big enough for cooperation."

She looked up.

A shooting star crossed the sky.

Moli made a wish and she wished for world peace.

***

When Tiansu woke up, the shamaness had gone. It was as mysterious as the way she had descended from the sky.

And no matter how the Khan implored, the divine chariot never replied with a sound again. He declared that, from then on, only shamanesses could assist future Khans.

In the following years, the Khan established a military system where every hundred soldiers made a squad, each squad had a leader, and every thousand made a battalion. They had also devised a plan for rewards and punishments and made use of logs for recording.

As Uncle Dazhe said, the grassroots in Ruoluoshui were indeed quite sweet, but Focat didn't seem to enjoy them.

Chapter 13

A cruise sailed up the Thames.

"Young lady, care to tell me why you are moping and so chap-fallen?" A silver-haired elder woman sat beside Moli with a cup of coffee in her hand.

Soft jazz played.

Moli pulled her thoughts back and hesitated. "Umm... what does 'moping' mean?"

"Well, it means feeling sad and lost," the woman offered.

"Oh, it's nothing. I was just..." Moli told her hands. "I was just thinking about a friend." She paused. "We'll probably never see each other again."

"That's not for you to say though, is it?" The woman thought. "You know what? My grandmother once said the very same thing as you. She had a good friend, a colleague. They were separated during World War II and briefly reunited after the war and parted. But it wasn't long before they got together again." She smiled. "I remember so many nights as a child. They snuggled in front of the fireplace, looking at flowers on the mantelpiece, sipping cocoa, chatting about old, sentimental love stories, reminiscing about the college hall where they used to work together." She sipped her coffee. "As long as we live, there is still hope."

Moli nodded, not knowing what to say.

She had just watched a video for a timeline of Chinese history, from the Battle of Zhulu to the fall of the Qing Dynasty. There was no mention of Rouran in that ten-minute video. Even the Northern Wei appeared for only five seconds.

Such a long history. Countless wars. So many lives lost.

Moli found herself fortunate to live in a China free of embroilment.

"I listened to your mother's presentation yesterday," the woman mused. "When we first heard that we were to produce PPE, we were so worried about securing the materials, designing the production lines, and the logistics." She took another sip of her coffee. "But where there's a will there's a way. No matter how far apart, no matter how confusing the time zone schedules are, together, we did it." She looked at Moli. "When everything settles down again, I'm thinking about revisiting the Penglai Pavilion on my next holiday. My husband teaches Japanese literature, and he is particularly fond of the *Penglai Song* by Kitamura Toukoku."

"Ah, Moli. Here you are." Maggie walked over, carrying her laptop. "Do you want to join the other children?"

Moli shook her head and stood up. "I'll go and use the washroom."

"Perhaps I can show you some photos of our last visit to the Penglai Pavilion. We were very fortunate to see the mirage," the woman suggested.

"Yes, I would love to see them," Moli said. She didn't sound excited at all.

"Remember to wash your hands carefully," her mother reminded her.

As soon as Moli had left, Maggie noticed that a small object had fallen out of her daughter's coat pocket.

A USB receiver.

Here you are.

She had been looking for it for her wireless mouse for almost an hour.

Maggie opened her laptop and plugged it in.

As she washed her hands, Moli saw the scar inside her palm.

Not a dream.

She looked at herself in the mirror and found nothing changed. But she knew that something had changed. She learnt that she could cry and be strong.

In the early morning, Edith woke up as soon as Moli slipped into bed.

Moli gave her such a hug that she seemed startled.

Then, Edith had suggested Moli take a bath. As she prepared the tub, she asked Moli the meaning of 'māo zhǎng fēng'. Moli told her that it means a wind soft and light like a cat's paw.

At eight o'clock, someone knocked on the door. It was Maggie.

It turned out that she had worked quite late and she didn't want to disturb them, so she had stayed in another room.

After a hurried goodbye, Edith went to catch her train.

Moli excused herself to go to the bathroom while Maggie logged on to Zoom.

She took out her phone and typed a message to her dad.

*Did you know that the Rourans used sheep
dung balls to count their soldiers?*

The message sent. She typed another one.

I miss you so much.

Moli clutched her phone and cried for a long time.
She resented the loss, yet she also regretted not cherishing.

***

Maggie brought Moli to her company's mobile office on the Thames. On their way to the pier, Moli searched about the history of Rouran and learned that the Shelun Khan had annexed several neighbouring tribes and reigned for nine years. He died in 410 CE after being defeated by the Northern Wei. And there was indeed a Chinese cultural relic called the 'Dragon Chariot of Ten Thousand Sages' that was stored in the Golden Dragon Museum in Bendigo, Australia.

Someone came into the bathroom. Moli dried her hands and went out.

"I don't want to play with plastic blocks! They take a thousand years to degrade!" a child whined.

"There's a difference between the attitude of 'whatever it takes' and 'whatever'!" another voice shouted. "The bloody social contract, like any other contract, has small print that says 'subject to change'! All of a sudden, people wallowed in walking their dogs, even those who don't have one!" Another voice.

"They look at others through distorting mirrors and magnifiers not knowing that they needed periscopes all the time!" Another voice.

"The NHS is not working as it should, the UK contact tracing is not working as intended, and it will cause great trouble if we still boast about it being a world-class healthcare system." Another voice.

"Do they really think that the Paris Agreement is a public lavatory that they could leave and visit as they wish? There was a time when other countries looked up to US leadership; now they see it as a joke. Do you know why the US failed? They failed because they have a 'cowboy' culture that lionizes risk-taking. Whether the US created the virus, they didn't cooperate to stop it."

So many voices.

Moli stood there, not knowing where to go.

A whistle shrilled.

"MAN OVERBOARD!"

"Bloody hell! There's a young lad in the water!" someone screamed.

Moli watched as people rushed onto the deck. In a split second, their movements stilled, the music faltered, slowed, and their shouts became staccato.

She saw a man passing her freeze. The dials on his wristwatch spun so fast that the watch face burst open.

"Moli!" Qiuniu appeared on the chandelier, its voice anxious. "Where is Eniac, the digital cloud?"

Moli searched her pockets as she ran to her seat. Her mother and the silver-haired woman were as still as wax figures and their bodies dissolved in air like chalk in storms.

Maggie's laptop flashed a purple screen. Moli saw the USB had connected.

"It's too late now." Another voice. "I knew something went awry when the orcas started attacking sailing boats, when Earth spins faster than usual, and when there is lightning in the Arctic."

Moli looked up. There was a cat with a long tail like a boa beside Qiuniu.

"What's happening?!" Moli asked, her voice full of desperation.

"What won't happen? From marble waterfalls to toxic electricity, all hell is breaking loose. Seems we have borrowed grave trouble." The cat fidgeted in mid-air, its tail twisting. "Fortunately, we still have the energy to store a snapshot of your history at this very moment. My name is Moxie. Follow me, human child."

Then Moli heard a roar. She saw a flash of golden light by the window. She ran onto the deck after Qiuniu and the flying cat.

Another roar.

Moli stopped.

There was...

There was a...

There was a dragon.

A dragon.

Its body stretching for miles, its golden scales gleaming, its gossamer whiskers floating, its claws strong...

How wakening the dragon roared!

How beckoning the dragon roared!

How invigorating the dragon roared!

Moli stood there, awed, as the rutilant Golden Dragon chanted. "Those who wish to escape, you shall decide if this world of yours is to reshape..."

***

James Walker scarpered home that morning and ran all the way to Blackfriars Bridge.

It lashed down and the wind was biting.

What have I done?! What have I done?!

A car passed, and a squashed Monster Energy drink can was thrown out.

Flashback.

"DO YOU HAVE ANY BLOODY IDEA WHAT DOES THE PHRASE 'UNLEASH THE BEAST' MEANS?" his father growled.

"DON'T YOU SEE! THEY TRY TO DIVERT OUR ATTENTION TO WUHAN SO WE NAIVELY FORGET FORT DETRICK! WHEN CHINA REACTED, THEY SAID IT WAS A FLU! THEY SAID NO NEED TO WEAR MASKS! THEY SAID WE SHALL HAVE HERD IMMUNITY! AND LOOK, WHAT HAPPENED! LOOK WHAT HAPPENED TO YOUR MOTHER! WHY ARE OUR TWITTER POSTS REMOVED? WHY IS DAVID ICKE'S FACEBOOK PAGE REMOVED? THEY DON'T TOLERATE OUR QUERIES BECAUSE THEY ARE AFRAID OF US KNOWING AND US TELLING THE TRUTH! THEY MADE US LAUGH AT CHINA! YET

WE CAN'T ACCOMPLISH WHAT THE CHINESE DID! WE ARE ON OUR OWN! WE ARE ALL DOOMED IF WE DON'T TAKE ACTION! IF WE DON'T SAVE OURSELVES!"

Since that day, his father had tin foil wrapped over everything in the house.

Unleash the beast...

"Noooo!" James kicked away the can and ran until his ribs burnt.

"THE PEOPLE WHO ARE FORCING LONDON INTO ANOTHER LOCKDOWN ARE THE SAME ONES WHO THREATENED TO USE LEGAL ACTION AGAINST SCHOOLS TO FORCE THEM TO REOPEN EARLIER! LOCKDOWNS ARE USELESS NOW! THEY ARE TO CREATE POVERTY! TEAR UP SOCIETIES! THEY ARE TO ELIMINATE HUNGER BY ELIMINATING US! AND LOOK WHAT A DISASTER HAPPENED WITH BREXIT! NO WONDER THE OTHER EU COUNTRIES DITCHED US! AT LEAST, FOR NOW, WE STILL HAVE CHLORINATED CHICKEN AND HORMONE-INJECTED BEEF BANNED, WHAT WOULD HAPPEN WHEN THERE IS NOTHING LEFT TO EAT! DO WE HAVE ANY CHOICES THEN?! DON'T YOU SEE! THEY SET THE GOAL! 'END HUNGER, 2030!' THEY ARE ENDING US! THEY CALL IT A 'NATURAL EXPERIMENT'! THERE IS NOTHING NATURAL ABOUT IT! THIS IS A PLANDEMIC!"

James couldn't seem to get rid of his father's words.

Things got worse after his father joined a group led by someone close to, or at least someone who claimed to be close to, David Icke. The WiFi was removed, the tap water stopped, the windows sealed, and James' phone confiscated.

"DON'T YOU SEE WHO IS BEHIND ALL THIS? THEY WANTED US TO HAVE NOTHING! NOTHING IN 2030! WE WILL OWN NOTHING! BUT BE OWNED! THE WORLD ECONOMIC FORUM BRAGS ABOUT IT! WE WILL OWN NOTHING! WE HAVE NO PRIVACY! HOW IS POLITICAL FREEDOM POSSIBLE IF THERE IS NO ECONOMIC FREEDOM?! THEY HAVE BEEN PLOTTING THIS! THE SHADOW GOVERNMENT! THE NEW WORLD ORDER! THOSE WHO CONTROL THE MONEY! THOSE WHO CONTROL THE MEDIA! THOSE WHO CONTROL THE PHARMA! THE TECH GIANTS ARE IN THIS! FIRST BREXIT, THEN THE PANDEMIC! HISTORY IS MESSED UP WITH HIS TORIES WITH THEIR HANCOCK HYPOCRISY! MILLIONS OF GOVERNMENT CONTRACTS GIFTED TO TORIES' FRIENDS AND CRONIES! THIS IS WHAT THEY CALL NO ONE LEFT BEHIND?! NONE OF THEM ARE LEFT BEHIND, AND ALL OF US WILL PERISH FOREVER! WE WILL ALL BECOME KNOCKOUT MICE! YOU SAW *HOLD-UP* WITH ME! WHY DON'T YOU UNDERSTAND?! THE WORLD IS MUCH MORE COMPLICATED THAN YOU THINK! I HAD A VISITATION ONCE! I SAW THE CORNWALL OWLMAN ONCE WHEN I WAS LITTLE! I ASKED FOR HELP! I CRIED FOR HELP AND HE WAS THERE! HE

MADE ME SEE! THERE IS NO GOD! NO ONE CAN SAVE US! NO ONE CAN SAVE US! ONLY US!"

His father shook him so dreadfully that day that afterwards he found weals on his shoulders.

"JAMES! OPEN YOUR EYES! STOP THAT NONSENSE! YOU CANNOT BE WHO YOU ARE NOT! YOU ARE A MAN! BE A MAN! WE NEED YOU! OR WHY DO YOU THINK DEAGLE LOWERED POPULATION PROJECTIONS THAT MUCH? SEVENTY PER CENT DOWN IN THE UNITED STATES! THE US WAS RANKED NUMBER 1 ON THE GLOBAL HEALTH SECURITY INDEX! IT IS A JOKE! WHY DO YOU THINK THE US IS DEMANDING INVESTIGATIONS IN CHINA, YET THEY DO NOT ALLOW W.H.O. INVESTIGATIONS IN THE US?! THE VACCINES ARE NOT GOING TO WORK! WHY DO YOU THINK PFIZER'S CEO CASHED OUT SIXTY PER CENT OF HIS STOCK?! DO YOU HAVE ANY BLOODY IDEA HOW MANY OF THE PHARMA COMPANIES HAVE BEEN FINED SINCE 2000 FOR VACCINES THAT DON'T WORK?! THE VACCINES WILL NEVER OUTPACE MUTATIONS! THIS IS APOCALYPSE! SOMEONE IS TRYING TO WARN US! THE 2012 OLYMPICS OPENING CEREMONY WAS TO WARN US! WE HAVE HELP! IF YOU JUST! IF YOU COOPERATE! MAN UP!"

NO!

James ran down the bridge, panting. He stopped, bent over, and threw up.

Where to now?

He did not have any masks left. He did not have anywhere else to go.

James reached into his pocket and felt the sharp edges of his keys.

Maybe he could go and work at a Timpson's after all.

Mother still in ICU...and father...and father...

He slumped on the embankment.

Mother still in ICU... And she could go to her reward this very second...

He remembered a bus driver in France who was beaten by passengers refusing to wear masks and who passed away...

BASTARDS!

What kind of reward is this?!

What kind of world is this?!

A cruise ship made its way along the river.

Music played. James only found it noisy.

He saw people socialising on that ship.

They looked happy. They smiled. They laughed.

They have their champagne, their diamond masks, their WFH, their games, their ten thousand hours, their mindfulness...

What have we got?

Our zero-hour contracts...overcrowded jails...care homes that no one cares about...

Some time ago, James had met someone on The Student Room. The bloke was chuffed because his dad had got him a PS5.

"And what does he do?" James asked. He had expected him to be an IT specialist of a sort.

"He's in pharma," the other end typed. "Sweden placed a big order for morphine and midazolam. You know, to ease the old with COVID off. They use Rivotril in France."

What sort of world is this?

James' mother caught the virus while working. She had to remind someone to wear a mask and was spat on.

BASTARDS! BASTARDS!

What sort of world is this?

He closed his eyes and sang a few phrases that he had read in a book.

A book he once loved and no longer believed.

Nothing happened.

His best memories did not come to his aid.

Death has three spellings: corpse, ghost, and memory.

His worst memories haunted him.

The only one who understands is lying in a hospital bed.

They might be easing her off now.

There is no more hope...

No hope...

What to do?

Humans lied. Algorithms misled.

No school. No work. No one who understands. No home to go back to.

Home...

It was home no more...

That morning, his father was sozzled.

Drunk again. Always drunk.

They had a row.

They always had rows.

And...

James looked up.

Far away, ravens fled the Tower of London.

Might it be a harbinger?

James looked down.

The river was surprisingly limpid, yet his reflection was blurred.

No hope.

No more hope.

James rubbed his eyes roughly and closed them. He thought he felt a strong gush of wind.

The very next second, he was in the water.

It was neither the long way down nor the quick way out.

It's over... It's over...

James heard a whistle and someone shouting, "MAN OVERBOARD"

How far can sound travel in water?

It's not over... It's not over yet...

"Hel...help..." James gasped for air. Water surged into his mouth, into his lungs. He tried to grab onto the slippery, slimy edges helplessly.

He yowled.

He kicked.

He grabbed.

He floundered...

He had remembered that his mother had once told him that King Henry III had kept a polar bear in the Thames.

His best memories flooded into his head.

Museum visits. School open days. Sketching lessons. Book clubs. Benny the beluga.

No father...and...no mother... It's over...

James shut his eyes and allowed his body to sink.

Yet he didn't. He felt solid ground under his feet.

How deep is the Thames?

James looked down.

There was...

There was a...

He stood on an Archelon. Its scutes were rough against his feet.

"I sensed troubled waters," he heard it say in a solemn voice.

I'm losing it. I'm losing it. Too many books. Too many fantasies. See what they did to you. See how they let you down, James thought as he retched and cried.

Hot tears riled with bitter bile and seething anger roiled with regrets.

Then a warm air bubble engulfed him.

***

Chitundu Mwikiza ended his piano practice on Yiruma's 'River Flows in You'.

He arranged his notes, closed the fallboard, and moved to the window side.

It was sunless that day, the clouds were heavy with languor.

His mothers were still at the hospital, working.

Even since their hospital started one-to-two nursing care, they seemed more motivated and much more exhausted.

He looked out of the window. Very few people lingered at South Bank in the downpour.

Kiza used to love living close to the Thames.

During summer, they would go and watch people skating under Waterloo Bridge. They would visit second-hand bookstalls and look at people practising and breakdancing at the Southbank Skatepark. His mothers would try all sorts of trinkets. They would take their time and wait for street art performers to complete a sand painting or visit Borough Market for snacks. They would stay out until the sun set around nine or ten in the evening.

And now, it is so deserted...

A raven came to his window, perching on its edge.

No.... He wasn't sure if it was a raven. It looked a little strange.

Kiza remembered the last time they had travelled.

Last year, a trip to Switzerland. The trip had done him good.

He had learnt so much, not only the languages but folklore and compositions by locally renowned pianists. They had also visited the observatory at Mont Soleil.

Kiza remembered one of their Airbnb hosts had mentioned a mythical creature in Alpine folklore; something called the 'Tatzelwurm' – a cat with a snake's body that can kill a human with poison in an instant. It reminded him of a mythical creature called Kongamato...and another called Mokèlé-mbèmbé.

Why is it that the Mokèlé-mbèmbé was called the Loch Ness Monster of Africa and the Loch Ness Monster not the European Mokèlé-mbèmbé?

The phone burred.

Kiza moved to the living room and picked it up. "Hullo?"

It was Mrs Kim, his piano teacher, calling to say that she might be late.

"Yes, I can take care of myself. I have been practising." Kiza ended the call.

It was too early for lunch, and he did not want to practise any longer.

He did not wish to make war with himself and his piano.

Music.

What can music do?

Music cannot save lives.

Music cannot even stave off the virus.

He had seen Dr Tedros responding to death threats and racial insults. He had seen him weeping over the ever-increasing COVID-19 death toll and confirmed cases.

Kiza began to regret his decision, yet it was too late to prepare for BMAT if he wished to secure an offer that admission cycle.

He looked out once again.

The leaden sky reminded him of the first time he had finished reading *The Three-Body* trilogy. He dared not look at the sky afterwards.

Aliens...

Are there aliens?

Could the virus have come from space?

During that summer in lockdown, he had attended an online summer school on space. There was a guest lecture delivered by NASA's Chief Scientist, who asked, 'almost one hundred metric tons of cosmic material fall on the Earth every day. Did the COVID-19 virus come from space or did it not? And how can we know?'

How can we know? How can we ever know?

Kiza had met a Chinese student on that summer programme; they worked on the same presentation topic on utilising space assets to prevent future pandemics.

His teammate was disheartened that the very same people who worked in scientific institutions like ESA said that the 'virus was a scheme by the Chinese to kill us all'. She also said, "And they talk about the 'province' of Wuhan not even knowing it is a city. They cite that non-peer-reviewed article on search engine results and diarrhoea. Yet very few talk about the questionable research practices it used and the misinterpretation of insufficient data. They have already reached their own conclusions, however unscientific that may be, however ridiculous that may sound. Ignorance beats science. Ignorance destroys all conscience."

We know so little of everything...

Are we not just a grain of dust in the entire universe?

Are we not just a single leaf in the entire forest?

Kiza remembered the Tree of Life sculpture at the British Museum. He looked out again.

A cruise ship made its way up the river.

There was someone on the bankside, looking at the water.

Kiza picked up a magazine, had a quick flip-through, and put it down.

He moved into the study; his mothers' collection of *Star Wars* action figures had gathered a thin layer of dust. Beside Luke Skywalker was an Australite Tektite, and a resin figure of a tardigrade. A friend had 3D-printed it for his fifteenth birthday.

Sometimes Kiza wished that humans could be as strong as tardigrades.

The vaccines...please, please make them work. Please don't let haste make waste. Please be thorough and rigorous. Let there be no mishaps, no side effects, no more blood clots. Let them resolve the allergy issues promptly. And please let there be enough vials and syringes. Please use worst-case scenarios like they would do when launching satellites. Please consider the worst worst-case scenarios.

He sang silently.

If praying helped, he could pray all day, and he would pray all day.

But it did not.

Kiza knew a girl who suffered from narcolepsy because of the Pandemrix vaccine. He dreaded to think what might happen if something went wrong in any steps of the production and delivery processes of any of the vaccines.

He looked up. There were piles of books in the study, books that belonged to his cousin: *Accounting for Slavery: Masters and Management, Jamaica Ladies: Female Slaveholders and the Creation of Britain's Atlantic Empire, Is God A White Racist?, Dead Aid, Heart of Darkness, King Leopold's Ghost.*

He picked one up and put it down again.

Congo.

His homeland he had never visited.

Am I accursed?

Kiza followed that train of thought for the millionth time.

It was rumoured that his great-grandfather had sold out his villagers to the rubber merchants of Leopold II; those who took away fingers, limbs, and heads when work was not up to standard. They...

What did they do?

Did they not kick away the ladder, did they not chop off the mast, did they not drain blood from trees, from mines, and from people who lived on those lands for thousands of years? Did they not lie, cheat, and steal? Did they not promise hope and yet only deliver coup d'état?

In coup they delivered.

And yet, did they not attempt to amend their wrongs? Did they not devise ambitious plans to alleviate poverty, to provide education? Did they not introduce project after project? Millennium Villages... Playpumps abandoned, broken, and unmaintained... Failed efforts these may be, but they were still efforts. Could they ever make up for the structural violence their people imposed or were still imposing? Could they ever make up for the abuses they had perpetrated? And how long would it take? A thousand years was not enough. They could try all they want, but, unlike flows of money, lives could never be returned.

Looks, remarks, attitudes, bitterness, and resentment.

His cousin told him she had seen more discrimination in her one-year MPhil at Cambridge than her three-year BA in London combined. She told him of someone she had met at a Political Economy seminar who aspired to work for the British intelligence agencies once he graduated. They discussed the Ebola outbreak at that time, and he had said, 'The best way of getting rid of the problem is to have a blockade and bomb the entire African continent.'

His mothers told him, even pulse oximeters give biased results depending on people's skin colour. Wasn't discrimination already built into their social, economic, and political systems? Do these not produce perpetual implications and cause everlasting damage? Even the impact of COVID-19 was highly ethnically and racially stratified.

Could he ever amend for the wrongs his great-grandfather did?

Kiza made his way to the window again and looked out. The sky had obnubilated.

His little nephew, aged four, had asked his mothers, "If laughter is the best medicine, then why don't we laugh to stop the virus?"

The same person Kiza had seen earlier was still standing close to the bankside. In the blink of a second, that person was gone.

Kiza rubbed his eyes, fearing he had made a mistake. He saw that person fleetingly, his arms flailing in the water. He had remembered his mothers' colleague...

Think! No, no time to think!

Kiza quickly moved into the corridor. There was no one there.

The neighbours had been hiding from them for fear of contracting the virus. The lift was out of order, the stairlift blocked by boxes of toilet rolls.

Bummer! The stairs, then!

He found the stairs and grabbed onto the handrail tentatively.

Slowly...slowly!

"Woooaaaah!" Kiza cried out.

A sharp decline and his wheelchair tipped.

***

As soon as she arrived at the platform, Edith had heard someone shouting.

A man without a mask was harassing an Asian lady, and he spat out the vilest words Edith had ever heard.

The lady ignored him for a while, but he carried on.

Then the woman turned and said, "Rebound!"

The man carried on and on.

Finally, the woman snapped. "Mister, who do you think you are? I have work to do. I have students to attend. Do your shouting and cursing save lives? They don't! They never do. But do you know what you *can* do? You can stop being such a covidiot and stop spreading your aerosol and save some oxygen for Earth!"

The station staff came to resolve the problem. Edith got on her train, feeling lost.

There was no one else inside.

She found a seat and hugged her backpack.

More shouting.

Too much shouting.

If only troubled individuals were as easy to spot as Boots.

Edith took out her earphones and played a song on her phone.

It was 'I Wish I Could Go Travelling Again' by Stacey Kent.

She'd remembered that once she and Hua and her father had visited Morris at Cambridge. They punted, they strolled, and they shared Fitzbillies buns.

Edith knew that Hua had never been too fond of sugary pastries, yet she had enjoyed their little jaunt.

'I wish I could go travelling again...'

How she longed to revisit the Nohoch Mul Pyramid.

The song continued as the train left the station.

Edith had known two Morrises; one who had always been intrigued by history, and another still living in her memories.

She missed him sorely.

Memories.

Memories of her mother in a hospital bed. Memories of her mother in her coffin.

Someone said 'a single death is a tragedy, and a million deaths a statistic'.

Yet it was not.

It was a tragedy replicated a million times, a disaster spread across countries, devastation as contagious as the virus.

It was a million obituaries, a million newly made headstones, a million times when tears were shed.

Statistics are human beings with the tears dried off.

Edith knew that Hua had set away money for Moli's education, only to withdraw some for Morris' funeral arrangements.

She knew that he had suffered a long case.

The symptoms were minor at first. Then there was dyspnoea, there was emphysema, there was sepsis, there was acute kidney injury and, in the end...multiple organ failures.

She wondered – no, she hoped – that if there was indeed Meng Po's soup then at least her brother could forget the pain.

"There is no learning curve for pain."

She recalled the words of the man they had met at the British Museum.

Edith felt a tightness in her chest. It pained her. It pained her to see Maggie. It pained her to see Moli.

The virus knew no pain; the virus knew no politics; the virus knew no boundaries; the virus knew no gender or race. Feisty fellows, not so feisty ones, those who went to the gym every day, those who didn't...

The virus had killed hope, it had seeped into humanity, and it had squandered solidarity.

And how many people with non-communicable diseases passed away because they did not receive timely treatments?

Even those who survived COVID might suffer from brain fog and lasting symptoms.

The song ended, yet the following didn't play.

Edith took out her phone.

There was no signal.

She tried to connect to her music app again. Still no signal.

Edith opened her WiFi settings after the train passed through a tunnel. There was no Great Western Railway's on-board network; the only option available was called 'Pandorai Network'.

She didn't connect, knowing there were malicious networks that stole personal information in public places.

Edith put away her phone and looked out of the window.

Scenery passed, farmland passed, clouds passed, and time passed.

Suddenly, the train jerked to a halt.

The brakes squealed on the track, and Edith almost bumped into the seat opposite.

What's happening?!

The train chuntered up the track and stopped at a station.

Possibly another signal failure.

Edith sat there and waited for the announcements.

But none came.

In the end, she hauled her backpack and got off.

There was no one on the platform except for a burly, unkempt man who sat on the waiting bench.

He held something in his right hand that resembled a walking stick. If Edith didn't know better, she might have thought it was a bludgeon. She looked askance at the man and remembered PCSO Julia James.

Troubled individuals.

A friend of hers worked as a call handler for contact tracing, and he cried every day after work. The job was stressful. People insulted him; people lied to him. Someone even said that she would 'track him down and fix him'. Yet, the most heart-breaking thing was that people who knew that they were positive or in close contact with others who tested positive still went out to work.

There were bills to be paid and bread to be earned.

Troubled individuals...

How many have lost jobs? How many have lost homes? How many have lost families and friends? How many have lost faith? How many have lost hope?

Then Edith remembered there were even fraudsters sending out phishing emails telling people they were eligible to apply for their vaccines then asking for their card details.

"Andre."

The man's calling pulled Edith back from her musings.

"Andre!" the man called again. "I've been waiting for you."

Must be another troubled individual, Edith thought. She approached the man with caution, remembering what had happened to Sarah Everard. "Mister, do you know what's wrong with my train?"

The man thought for a while. "Yes and no."

"I don't quite follow you."

"I am aware of the trouble, and yet only you have the solution. Edith Orozco," the man said, his eyes searching hers, "I have been waiting for you."

"For me?" Edith eyed him dubiously.

"Yes." The man stood up.

He had a larger build than Edith observed. "My name is Aitor." He paused. "But people also call me *basajaun*. Now, if you will follow me," he gestured, "your alternative transportation is here. The time is here for you to travel again."

Edith turned and looked.

For a second, she doubted her own eyes.

There was...

There was a...

There was a Leonardo da Vinci's helicopter.

***

Somewhere in London.

A grand hall.

A man in a smoking jacket stood beside a window.

There was green carpet in the room.

Music played.

Wagner.

Such a magnificent edifice.

With its 1,000 rooms, 100 staircases, the niches, the brackets, the statues, the pillars, and the panorama of Thames.

The man looked out of the window.

He still considered architecture the queen of the arts, side by side with music.

There were a large Ferris Wheel and a pyramid structure in the distance.

How he longed to take a ride on the Giant Ferris Wheel in the Prater in Vienna as a winner...

Perhaps later he would redesign this city.

Nein.

He grinned. He would redesign them all.

There was a silver-plated book, with his initials, on the nightstand.

A mannequin stood nearby with a dress on it.

It was his favourite dress of hers, the black one with roses at the neckline.

He touched the dress and felt its velvety softness.

It felt nice to his fingertips.

It felt nice to be back.

He was back.

He was back!

Life down there was as bleak as paintings of Zdzisław Beksiński and smelt as olid as chlorine, phosgene, and mustard gases.

Brought back from the dead...

He once laughed at someone's obsession with esoteric black magic, necromancy, catoptromancy, and ancient paganism.

But he was back! Brought back from the dead, indeed!

The music stopped and he turned.

"The UK is a liberal democracy at its core with a long history adhering to international legislation," someone said inside a large, black-looking glass mounted on the wall.

Such hackneyed discourse.

Is this the land of hope and glory?

Was there any other nation who prepared the way for its commercial conquests more brutally than England did by means of the sword, gunfire, and cannons? Was there any other nation who defended such conquests more ruthlessly?

Winners write history. Winners dictate the rules. To the victor belong the spoils.

He always had a *hassliebe* with Britain.

"Hell-o World!" The mirror lit up and the image of a smiling skull appeared.

He walked over.

"Hi, there! My name is Pandorai, personal pronouns she, him, its, and the Almighty Terminator!"

"Who are you?" He examined the mirror with his fingers.

"I am your new-generation, state-of-the-art virtual assistant. I'm your CIO, CFO, CDO, COO and your Chief Impact Officer. I'm here to help so you can focus on what matters most. I can do many things all at once. I make calls, set alarms and reminders, arrange meetings, manage your smart appliances, play music, book opera tickets, run your house, do your grocery shopping, diddle your tax returns, cover up your malfeasances, execute your liquidations, personalise your war plans. You name it, and I nail it. I'm your one-stop shop for all machinations and despotism at your fingertips! What's better? You can also go incognito with your skulduggery. Never be bothered by leaked emails or slanders by previous lovers and kiss and tell. Never feel the need to use a telephone again—"

"No telephone?" He was intrigued. "Then how can I command my troops?"

"Have you not heard?" the machine said. "Tweeting is the new way of governing."

"Tweeting? Like this?" He whistled, mimicking the barn swallows from his childhood.

"No. Not like that." The mirror made a naughty face. "Public relations matter today, and so do innovation and leadership. But don't you sweat. I'm your all-in-one confidant. Oh, also, remember, Finland is not a part of Russia."

Gut, he thought. At least the Soviets had failed to take over the world.

"Enabled by machine learning, I can anticipate what you need before you even realise. Just ask, anytime, anyplace. Together, we can spell the end of the human race. Let us make it a year that people will talk about...if they survive! To get started, please tell me your name," the machine said without stopping.

He cleared his throat. "Adolf."

"Righto. Welcome, Adolf. Would you like to tell me your gender? Or do you prefer not to say?"

"What's more to tell? I am man."

"Methinks you might have missed an article there. Anyways, shall we proceed?"

A bioroid butler came in, bearing a silver tray, on it a bone-white ring shaped like a skull.

"Now, for better communication purposes, please wear this ring," the mirror suggested.

He put it on tentatively. "What is it for?"

The mirror said, "This is specially made for you. Adolfie, how do you want to start your conquests?"

He felt more confident in speaking English, "Magic mirror, on the wall, who is the wisest one of all?" he asked, quoting a line from his favourite movie.

"Here are the vices of men: arrogance, rapacity, untrustworthiness, iniquity, exploitation, partiality–"

"No! I meant the wisest one!"

"Searching..." the machine said, "pictures showing vices and men."

He was peeved. "Show me the news, then!"

The screen flashed, and headlines flowed.

News.

Huh.

Could there be anything new?

The Phaeacians roamed still.

The press still played lackey to the ones who controlled.

Generations duped by the pernicious press and its string-pullers...

This much he had expected, yet he did not expect the news.

What was going on?

Germany paying reparations again.

The US in chaos.

The USSR was long gone.

Terrorists attacked Vienna.

Animals euthanised in zoos and fed to other animals.

People laughing when flooding in Germany kills hundreds.

Hundreds of tonnes of nuclear wastewater on its way into the Pacific Ocean.

Thousands of acres of forests destroyed by bush fire.

Millions of minks exterminated.

A world in mire and strife.

Death seeking its prey everywhere.

He stood there and thought.

Those who have insulted Mother Nature...

Distress, misery, and disease are her rejoinders.

And the culling has finally begun...

It only proved that the world could tolerate casualties – quite a lot, in fact, and in the US especially.

A news item played.

Someone said on the screen, 'Yes, China protected lives, yet we safeguarded our freedom and the things that we hold dear and uphold with dignity...'

Another said, 'What we didn't model for is that people would choose to go to a party if they knew that they were positive and that people would fake negative test certificates. We didn't model for TV hosts cutting up masks on air, presidents insulting public health experts in press conferences, and federal governments shilly-shallying. We did model for scenarios where people might be loath to wear masks and wash their hands more frequently, but we did not model for people who smear bus handles with their saliva or people who drink and inject Clorox. We also failed to model for city mayors who violated staying-at-home plans, state governors attending parties, and a Speaker of the House of Representatives who liked to have her hair done in-salon against her better judgement. And we certainly did not model for antics such as police raiding whistle-blowing scientists' homes in Florida. Government's first duty is to protect us, not ruin our lives...'

He could not refrain from laughing out loud.

Freedom.

What do any of them know about freedom?

Are they even capable of finding the road, no, the entrance to freedom?

These fatuous minds could only be herded onto the thoroughfare to serfdom.

Apparently, the canaille has already been reduced to total subjection.

And what do the dregs of society know about dignity?

Even Volkswagen has brought shame to German workers.

Opportunities were now presented to him. He always seized them at the right moments. The world apparently needed a new leader and he was up to the challenge again.

"Who is the great power today?" he asked.

News reeled.

China's Tiangong Space Station...

China's Wolfskrieger...

China's strong economy...

China's lead in RCEP...

China's Chang'e 5...

He was certain that they had misspelt 'change'.

China...

He snickered.

Propaganda is a farce nowadays.

When was China ever a wolf?

When was the last time China harried anywhere?

When was the last time China air-raided anywhere?

When was the last time China subverted foreign governments anywhere?

And who is the real coyote?

"Show me the US Armee." His German accent seeped into his speech.

The mirror obeyed.

"Does China have military bases all around the world? Does China have more than two hundred biological warfare laboratories in Georgia? In Ukraine? In the Middle East? In Africa?" he asked.

"Nope, don't be fooled by those Doomsday Howlers," the machine replied. "Amerikakania is the greatest dirty force in the world today!"

"Ameri...kakania... Like Robert Musil's *kakania?* The Poo-poo-land?"

"That's right!" the mirror laughed. "Amerikakania is the *ne plus ultra* of shitty negative freedom. People there are free to be mangled to death by the police. They are free to shoot others into sieves. They are free to live without utilities, and they are free to ask for no handouts. They are free not to care for others and to be depraved. Even the ex-President cannot speak freely. They are free to be trammelled and tossed around like a salad and to dissolve in the melting pot. They are free to die like maggots. Who's the man without qualities and where's the State that is shackled to corpses now? The Average Joe will make Amerikakania greatly boring again! Yet you! You can leave so much more for Germany other than *Das Auto* and *autobahn!*"

He laughed.

The US still had a large, active armee and strong walls around its borders, but look what had happened.

The higgledy-piggledy ship of democracy sees another mutiny as it crashes onto an iceberg and all their pretence of not sinking and drowning is killing them. Did the dunderheads and riffraff onboard really think they could discover a 'great man' through elections?

There is a better chance of seeing a camel passing through the eye of a needle.

Such donnybrook and trumpery.

The city on the hill is shining just as the King Shit of Turd Mountain is burning.

They did indeed handpick their own author of danger and finisher.

They did indeed die by suicide.

It was the US who brought the Influenza that depleted Germany post-World War I.

Revenge is indeed better served with retributive desserts and poetic justice indeed sounds quite nice to the ears.

Now that they were scraping the barrel, he was glad that Providence favoured him again. He could finally make Linz a world city.

"Everybody knows that Trump's a dog and a dead *dawg*." The mirror seemed to be able to read his mind.

"He does look like one. He looks like a pug," he commented.

"A pug it was." The mirror laughed indignantly.

"How did he die? Another assassination?" he asked.

"*Oooooh*, we are talking at cross purposes here. Trump's the dog of a British painter called William Hogarth. He's quite well known for his satirical pieces, and he painted better than you. But hey, Adolfie, no one is perfect. A Donald of all trades means a master of none. Yet, you are remembered forever as the true anomaly with no virtue and the world's most famous loss leader and arch-fiend in the annals of history! Is that fair?"

"Tell me what to do. Tell me how to *win*."

The mirror buzzed. "Strategy is about deciding what not to do. Adolfie, everything you did was bloody brilliant. You are Michelangelo; what you need to do is not to do more. You need to knap and chip away the marble, so David comes out of it. You need to burn all your bridges, including Ponte Vecchio. You need to lessen, dislimn, and approach it with calamity. *Und* I believe we possess all the resources and creativity necessary to construct all the Marble Arch mounds in your marble cities for your *lebensraum*."

"Show me my troops," he commanded.

"Here are some options that I have handpicked for you based on your preferences and past user history. Werewolves: wolf-like robots that tear and spear...just like your good old panzer units."

Squads of fur-less, grey-metal wolves burst into the room, their paws sharp like cutlasses.

He nodded. "What else?"

"Legion Orange: eagle-like drones equipped with Agent Orange and mini doodlebugs that spray and foray ready at aerodromes across the UK..."

He looked out of the window, where thousands of mechanical eagles painted orange with three-metre-long wings soared.

"Stingrays, standing by in the Thames." The machine displayed an image. "These are remotely operated underwater vehicles that allow you to kill at will. I have also prepared obsequious bioroid butlers and metallic maids that guard you and serve your everyday needs. Never worry about assassins again."

He straightened his uniform and nodded with satisfaction.

"Armageddon has come, or is it the orbific Day of the Rope? Solidarity is falling and failing." The mirror cackled again, "I can make the world your Etch a Sketch. Let's gate crash the marriage supper of the lamb! Let's pierce every heart at this fin-de-epoch! This will be the *greatest* week since creation! We can make the globe a Jackson Pollock! Let's make the Final Solution a grand finale! Let's B3W the world. Let's bomb, blast, and burn each and every city! Oh, yass we can!"

"Very well," he said.

Humans betrayed, better let machines foray.

The time he had spent down there, he had learnt well.

The gist of modern warfare is efficiency and gamut.

Why strafe cities when there are quicker means to extirpate?

Why feed the pauper when machines could create?

The end is nigh.

This time, he would build his own Weltanschauung and his new Herrenvolk.

This time, he would have his rightful place in the Walhalla.

He trembled with excitement.

He was determined to win this time, and this time this world would not be enough.

"And who are my worthy opponents?" he asked the mirror. "Stalin?"

"No."

"Churchill, then?"

"No."

"Then it must be Roosevelt the Jew!"

"Here they are."

The mirror flashed several dossiers.

He grinned once again.

Not even Charles de Gaulle!

Children.

Kinder.

And not even normal, healthy children.

Inferior children.

He would, for sure, win this time, for he had learnt.

The non-Aryans may well learn the German language; they may well adopt a German lifestyle; they may even cast their votes for a German political party...

Yet.

The only good non-Aryans are the dead ones.

Ten out of ten times.

He would not tolerate their presence and infestation for long.

Someone knocked.

"Enter," he ordered.

A man taller than him came into the room and saluted him. "My Führer, it is my great honour to assist you on this mission. Together, may we create glory for our countries."

He didn't even eye the man. "Please tell me more about your past records."

The man gave a lopsided smile. "My Führer, are you aware that the heart is among the strongest muscles in the human body? And do you know human infants have the highest percentage of body fat among all mammals' infants? I have been called the 'Josef Mengele of the East', a title I consider below me for once I held a world record for the greatest number of autopsies performed and I have vivisected even more. I understand art as something that is creative and inimitable. I have pioneered many studies and have conducted many experiments with a rigorous, scientific approach on many test subjects, on children, elders, men and women alike. Oh, and also infants. You are an artist, my Führer, and I am a scientist. And science is an art. *Ars Moriendi.* The art of dying. This time, allow me to assist you to win with science."

After a considerable pause, finally, he turned. "Very well. I bestow on you the title of the first Honorary Aryan in my new Reich."

Chapter 14

"Copy made? Check. Solar protocols activated? Check. Gravity altered? Check. Ozone layer strengthened? Check. Check, check, check. Phew. That was a close call. I have not been pressed for time like this since the Kindertransport."

James heard someone talking in his stupor.

It didn't sound human.

So, this is how it is, he thought. He no longer felt cold and drenched.

Too soon to accept.

"What will happen to Maggie?! What will happen to everyone?!" a girl's voice urged.

"We have tucked them safely away in the Niflheim and no one has been left behind. As for the decision, that, I'm afraid, is yours to make. Of course, we will have to wait for the others." The inhuman sound continued, "Speaking of which..."

Footsteps rushed in.

"Sorry we're late," a fruity voice said.

"Aitor, you being late is as rare as a triple Jovian eclipse," the inhuman sound replied without inflection.

"Is Confucius back yet?"

"Not yet. They might encounter turbulence when aerobraking. I've just readjusted the settings."

"Aunt Edith!" he heard the girl shouting. "Aunt Edith!"

"Oh! My good grief! Moli! Do you know what is happening? I'm totally lost."

Another voice. A young grown-up.

James tried to fight off the fog hovering over his mind as the girl explained.

There was too much to process, and she gabbled so fast.

He only heard fragments.

An exhibition...and sons of dragon...a turtle...a snake.... A question... two doors... Time slip... A shaman and a bronze eagle...the cloud...a digital service...no, a digital cloud...war...chariot...strategy...USB...ultrasound.

It did not make sense at all.

Must be a dream...

Footsteps were going away.

"What I don't understand is why here and why now, when everything is so... chaotic, and why such unpropitious timing?" the inhuman voice pleaded.

"Perhaps it's better this way. The humans still have not grasped that the only certainty is uncertainty and a symptom of the desire for certainty among vagaries is likely to fuel the revival of extreme nationalism and scapegoating. Imagine if he came up in their world now, how many would have been fooled and incited by his big lies again. I am more concerned about Pandorai. People can pander to others' agitation and inveigle others' enmity, but they are still mortals. The AI brings out humans' innermost trepidation and desires to no end. This evil day cannot be put off. We can only hope that the pandemic awakens and uplifts the human spirit once again."

The voices left the room, drifting away as a thin scrim of fog clogged his mind...

Or worse...I am comatose. Disembodied.

Yet James felt his throat burning, his eyes watery, and his body aching as he regained consciousness.

Then he felt something tickling his nose.

Something soft and fluffy.

James snapped open his eyes. In his milky vision, he saw a cat's face.

It was so close that its whiskers tickled him.

"Welcome aboard, James Walker," it hissed. "May I address you as James? Or do you prefer 'J'?"

He was stunned.

What shocked him more was that the cat floated in mid-air, its snake-like long tail coiled up like a chameleon's.

"Egad!" James bounced up, almost knocking over a globe. "Crikey! Is this *Life on Mars* or what?!"

"I would love to show you the Red Planet someday. But right now, we have more pressing matters at hand." The cat had a gold torc with jade and serpentine beads on its neck. On top of its ears there were elderflowers.

In a blink of a second, the cat was gone.

James regained his woozy foothold and looked around. He did not know why his clothes were dry and he found himself standing, barefoot, in an extensive library.

Wherever he was, he felt that he was inside something living, yet he could also hear engines chugging.

There were all sorts of bizarre objects inside that library.

A brougham...no. A jalopy of a Ford T Model but with a wood horsehead in front. Strange clothing, accessories and sundries that he had never seen before. More torcs on display. A mannequin with a British Warm and a Sutton Hoo helmet. A Wooton desk with three pouncet boxes on top. A pair of stout-looking leather boots in a glass cabinet. Tomes of old, yeasty books cheek by jowl and reams of vellum on shelves. A Terracotta soldier with a Fiske's Reading Machine in his hand and a giant book wheel that spins on itself besides him. Amphoras and a thurible. And there was a glass armonica and a hurdy-gurdy...and musical instruments on the wall he could not name. There were colourful ropes that he recognised as the Inca Quipu. There was a wheelchair in the corner. It looked like the wood Gendron that James' grandfather had once used after being maimed in World War II.

His feet felt cold against the wood floor.

Then James remembered where he had placed his sneakers.

He approached the glass cabinet with the pair of long boots and peeked inside. There were two initials carved on each boot top, 'G' and 'W', and a metal plaque that said 'For the Father of Our Country'. A rusty cotton weigh-up scale sat on top of the glass panel.

"You wouldn't be so interested in them if you knew what they were made from," a voice susurrated.

"Or *who* they were made from," another voice purred.

James spun around, his breaths maddening.

There was no one in the room.

"Here are your shoes." The cat/snake appeared, its tail grabbing his sneakers. "You should thank Aitor for taking a detour and picking them up. Nothing is as comfortable as an old shoe, right? Not that I have much experience of or need for footwear."

He had a better look at the cat. It had cat-like front legs and the slender body of a boa. Its fur had the palette of a boa as well. He noticed that it had a small jade ring on the tip of its tail.

The cat watched him as he put on his shoes unsteadily. "Would you care to join us for some tea while we wait? We will crack on with the details later."

James swallowed and nodded. He followed the creature and passed into a corridor. Then he saw a door; it had the most exquisite golden *rilievo* emblazoned on it and there seemed to be the sounds of waves splashing behind it.

He moved closer to inspect.

"This way, please. That's the Elysian Fields," the cat urged him. "Tell me, J, where do you think the virus came from? Do you consider it schemed and humanmade?"

"I...I dunno." He gave an honest answer.

In his befuddled state, James no longer knew whom and what to believe. For a few seconds, he wondered if cats were indeed aliens who spied on humans on Earth.

"Good. Thinking is a tool that we wield, not an influence we surrender. Right thinking is like a mental game of chess where you play against yourself, but also as a spectator and an adjudicator. You need to continually challenge yourself with the sources of your knowledge and their modalities. Progress is made when one acknowledges what one does not know and cannot be certain of, considering that humans always tend to overgeneralise and extrapolate. For instance, you tend to call everything that hangs in the sky and shines a 'star'. But are they really? A planet is certainly not a star. And, my J, you might be surprised to hear that shooting 'stars' are no stars either..."

James only nodded; he had no idea why this conversation was taking place. No, he doubted everything he had seen and heard since he had opened his eyes.

"Now, if you consider the virus a humanmade weapon, when predicaments arise, especially at a global level, do you concur that we have to ask some questions? Namely, which countries might have the resources and personnel to do this, and which countries have a track record of experimenting with new weapons on their own soil and on foreign ground? Let us call this fictitious 'Country A' for simplicity. Another important question might be that, if the virus was humanmade, who would benefit?"

"Umm...the pharma companies...the IT industry...the gaming and video-streaming firms...umm...and China."

"Did it really? So that Chinese children are bullied and ragged on at schools around the world? So that Chinese people are pilloried by others in their workplaces and their everyday lives around the world? To have cartoonists defacing the Chinese national flag and for stigmas to wrongfully mark the bodies and souls of Asian populations forever? Might it be too high a price to pay for some single-digit growth figure? And would you care to tell me how China gained more specifically? Did it loot anywhere or did it despoil anywhere given the mayhem?"

"No. Umm...They...they exported a lot when the supply chains in other parts of the world were disrupted...and when other economies were in lockdown..." James said, recalling a conversation he had overheard.

"Quite right. Would you agree that the Chinese economy picked up because it supplied goods and services, the masks, the PPE, when the Chinese factories were working flat out to support other countries to fight the virus?"

James remembered a neighbour who went to work in China and had been kind enough to mail him a package of masks in May.

"Now, imagine if the Chinese government had dismissed the virus as just a flu, or if the other countries were less altruistic, what do you think would happen then? Could it be that you are all fingers and thumbs with the virus on all fronts and there is no one to step into the breach? People who have never been to China claim to be 'Chinese experts', and people who have never learnt a single lesson in virology now have a say in where the virus came from. J, what is so destructive about conspiracy theories is not that people cannot distinguish between facts and lies, but that people are presented with different 'facts'. They eat into trust. Like the Internet, it splinters; it divides; it splits; it amplifies hate and its effects."

James sighed. "Maybe. I...I don't know. If it's humanmade, it might have been leaked..."

The cat stopped and wheeled around to face him. "Many epidemiologists and scientists claimed that the virus could only come from nature, and if a quarter of them still stand by their professional code of conduct, what do you make of the situation then?"

"Er...then nature must...it must be her way of...taking matters into her own hands..."

"So, to leave wildfires unattended, oil tankers unsupervised, animals exterminated, and flora destroyed? Do you think it is wise to stop air pollution by creating mask pollution? And have you personally met any of the Aqua and Terra spirits to voice such a stronghold? Have you humans not always narrowly assumed that when the Doomsday Clock advances to midnight, nature's Elfmeter will kick off? Has anyone asked nature if it was indeed her intention to cause the current, unchecked situation? You only see nature with your false mirrors, but what is essential is invisible to the eyes. You don't realise how privileged humans are. Gravity is a privilege. Tell me, J, do you know that there is no word for 'nature' in Mayan? When you create a name for 'nature', you separate yourselves from whatever is out there. When you make a categorisation, you distance yourselves from unity. Why do you suppose that you humans always force an 'it' and 'us' dichotomy?"

"I...don't know." James took a deep breath.

Why?

Why had he never asked himself these questions?

"You can start at least with wanting to know. Is it not because there are so many unknowns out there that humans need to explore? *Non est ad astra mollis e terris via.* There is no easy way from the Earth to the stars. Just like self-discovery. My dear J, the principle of least effort no longer works. There will be confusion; there will be opposition, there will be noise. There is no coming to consciousness without trouble and pain and toil. There will be 'Oh shit!' moments and there will be 'Eureka!' moments. Planetary systems are complex systems, and sidereal problems are wicked problems. Answers will not come to you; you need to seek them out. The sky is no longer the limit. You need to decolonise your minds. You need to stop the separation."

He followed the cat into the room at the far end down the corridor.

There were two other humans in there.

James was relieved to see them – an Asian girl and someone with short, bright lime coloured hair. They were sitting around a coffee table, having tea.

It smelled like jasmine tea.

Mother liked...no....Mother likes jasmine tea. And father likes Walkers crisps.

James closed his eyes.

"I hope you enjoy my Skyview Lounge," the cat said. "If you are uncomfortable with the altitude that we are currently at, I can ask the Captain to find another mooring point."

James opened his eyes once again. He only noticed then that this room did not have any walls or flooring, but transparent glass overlooking the London skyline. The glass had no seams.

He saw cars and trains unmoving. And he saw an aeroplane, suspended in the distance as well. Then he saw the Shard, under his feet.

It was so small, small like the miniature Eiffel Tower paperweight his father had tin foiled.

Must be a dream.

"Allow me to introduce," the cat said, as its tail literally snaked onto James' left shoulder, hugging him somehow. It was warmer than he expected. "This is James Walker from Earth. Oh. I must have made a lapse." It smiled. "Pleased to meet you. I am

Moxie the Ninth." Its tail shook with his hand. "I will leave you, earthlings, for some small talk for now."

Moxie the Ninth... James bit his cheek on the inside. It hurt.

Not a dream...

But can a comatose person feel pain?

He was rather flustered.

"Umm..." the person with lime-coloured hair stood up. "I'm Edith, and this is Moli. We...we are...from Earth as well," she said, looking completely nonplussed.

"Yea. I figured that much." James laughed a little.

The first time in days – no, months.

"Sorry..." Edith smiled with a hint of discomfiture. "It's quite a mind-boggling...situation that we got ourselves into. Just...just when I convinced myself that there is no magic."

"Ha! Magic! Things you cannot explain yet, you call them 'magic' and sweep them under the carpet and pretend that all is well." A harsh voice echoed in the room. "Perseus wore a magic cap so that the monsters he hunted down might not see him. You draw the magic cap down over your eyes and ears as a make-believe that there are no monsters. What a magic touch indeed!" The voice petered out.

"Er...well," James hesitated. "And you are...you are her aunt?" He looked at the girl.

"Yes. We are family by connection," Edith said. "Do you fancy a cuppa? Some jasmine tea perhaps? This is exactly when we should keep calm."

He joined them. There was a large knapsack on the seat beside his.

"Dear passengers, welcome aboard. Your Captain is speaking. I am Dapan de Sichuan," a chirpy voice echoed in the room. "While we wait, here is a little quiz to pass some time: what will alien penguins say if they discover Earth for the first time?"

Passing away...easing off... James could not help but let his thoughts stray again.

The girl, Moli, spluttered. "No, no, you don't understand! Aunt Edith, I opened it. I opened a door with the letter 'i' on it! And the USB! I left it so Maggie..."

James beseeched, "Can anyone PLEASE tell me what ON EARTH is going on?"

The girl looked at him with worry in her eyes. "It's really complicated."

"Well, say it! So we're not wasting any more time!" he said, a little too brusque, a bit too impatient.

The girl began to talk.

James understood every single word she said, but they made sense individually and made no sense at all together.

"Are you telling me that I ended up here only because you opened a wrong bloody door?!" James demanded.

"Haha! The humans! Always so eager to draw conclusions, and yet you always draw the wrong ones. Fault lines run so deep with your thinking and mentality," the same voice sneered again. "You look at the mud then you conclude there is spontaneous generation; you learn a bit of maths, and you conclude that the Earth is in the middle of everything, then you burn Giordano Bruno; you study the gecko, and you assert there can be no Spider-man! Is ignorance indeed bliss or a curse? Go read some Hume! You mock what you don't understand. You make fun of what is different even though you are only 0.01 per cent different from each other. Why do you have to be such nincompoops? Why do you have to be such *terrible simplificateurs*! Thinking you know it all? You don't even understand cloud shapes and you can't even distinguish what properties are inherent to metals." The gruff voice continued, "Little rug rat. My friend asked a question. You should show some courtesy and make an effort to engage with the conversation."

"Yazi?" The girl looked around. "Is that you? What should we do now? How are we going to save our world?"

"That is the very question that you should ask yourselves. Now, tell me, what would alien penguins say when they first discover Earth?"

They looked at each other, discomposed.

The door opened, and a black boy entered on the antique Gendron wheelchair.

"They would say," the boy said determinedly, "that with so little ice cap on the poles, this planet could not support intelligent life forms."

"That's right!" the chirpy voice said, "so all the better to use evidence-based thinking."

The boy's eyes met James' for a second, and he seemed relieved.

"Is that a Rebec you got in the library?" he asked. "Could I try to play it later? I've never seen one before. And can I also take a look at the Wimshurst machine?"

Moxie floated into the room and looked around. "Now that you are all here – Edith, James, Kiza, and Moli, check, check, check, check – we better get started." Its tail wriggling, it said,

"Where should I start? Without delving into the technical gobbledygook, how about bad news or good news first?"

"I would very much like the good news," James said.

We are all dead. This is a dream. I am moribund and disassociated, he thought.

"Very well," the cat nodded, "if this is agreeable to all?"

They nodded.

"When humans are stressed, you tend to mistake dreams for reality. But this is not a dream, nor are you in a coma, nor are you all dead." Moxie paused. "The good news is that your world is about to end, and you have one chance to save it. Only one." Its tail coiled up like a tape measure. "The bad news is that it will not be easy, and it is no task for the faint-hearted. But first things first. Let me ask this. Are you going to save your world? If you are not interested, just say so. We might as well grab some sycamores and damsons, and have fun from our ringside seats."

"Of course!" Kiza exclaimed. "My mothers...they are saving people's lives!"

"Are you sure you want to save this world of yours? Is it worth saving? Worth saving at all?" the cat hissed. "Non-action is also action."

"We must!" Edith said strongly. "So many lives at stake!"

"Oh, but how can people die if they have never lived?"

"What do you mean that they have never lived?" Moli almost cried. "Is our world rolling back to the original state?"

"Umm...not yet, but it may well be," the cat hissed. "And are you sure that you are going to save your world? No second thoughts?"

"No!" they said together.

"But what would happen if we fail?" Kiza asked. "What is the worst-case scenario?"

Moxie held James in its jewel-green eyes and asked, "Have you never wanted to undo time? Not even once? And I believe you know the answer already, Kiza." The cat paused. "This time, you will all be strong, although you may no longer take up the form of a *Homo sapiens per se*. Something more practical, more resistant to extreme conditions. Perhaps you might need to forgo some of the aesthetics as well. But you will acquire the ability to survive lethal UV radiation. Weren't you quite partial to the idea before?"

Moli saw Kiza's eyes opening wide. "So, if we fail, we will become...tardigrades?"

"Not quite," Moxie smiled. "If the other party succeeds, he may choose to paint a rather sordid picture, so to speak."

"Oh!" Edith tensed up somehow. "And who are we competing against?"

"We will wait for the person in question to make his first formal public appearance." Moxie waved its tail and its laugh jarred. "It will be grand. That's his style. Coming back to our question at hand, are you still determined to save your world now? No third thoughts?" It hissed. "The worst happens when you make a decision, reverse it, and later you regret it. Why waste everyone's time and energy? I very much dislike those who go back on their word."

"Of course not!" Kiza said vehemently.

"No fourth, fifth, and sixth thoughts?" the cat hissed again.

For a second, James was unsure if these creatures were there to help them or if they were there to enjoy a show.

"No!" they replied in unison.

"Are you in this together?!"

"Yes!"

"Good." The cat waved its boa-like tail. "For I will be disappointed if you didn't put up a fight and buckle down." It smiled. "Now that we have reached a consensus – Dapan, let's embark."

"*Yaode*." The chirpy voice echoed. "We should be there in...0.48 seconds."

Before they responded, as fast as PowerPoint slide changes, the scenery under their feet was replaced by that of the British Museum.

James had been to the museum many times, yet he had never seen its aerial view. The glass roof now looked like a slice of apricot Danish in green.

"Now, let's see." Moxie pressed the jade on its torc with the tip of its tail. "Where is my encryption key?"

They watched in awe as holograms of world-famous landmarks and their Ley Lines appeared and rotated around them.

"No, not the Mustatil Monuments. No, not the Pentagon. Not the Forbidden City. Not the Pyramid of the Sun either. Wait... Let me order by clause."

They saw the cat typing in mid-air. "Here, the UK, Greater London, Bloomsbury, British Museum... Eureka!"

"Wow!" Kiza looked down as the green sphere on top of the museum swirled open.

"Now, Confucius, it's your showtime," Moxie said as it typed more with its agile paws. "I've unlocked the security system."

"Much obliged, Moxie."

They saw something bungee jump into the museum.

A bird.

It was the size of a crow, black feathers with grey and white streaks down its wings and shiny speckling on its neck. A pair of long, thin feathers extended from each side of its tail with teardrop ends.

The bird also had a pair of aviator goggles on its head.

"Let's switch our POV." Moxie typed, and a window akin to a CCTV monitor appeared in the air.

They watched as the bird swooped down and glided into the museum with ropes in its claws, then found its way to the Rosetta Stone.

The protection case was no longer there, and the bird adroitly tied the ropes around the slab.

"All set now," they heard the bird say.

"Hold on a second," the chirpy voice that belonged to Dapan said. "Let's take it slow and easy."

They saw the ropes tighten and the stone was hauled up, all the way back to the Skyview Lounge.

"Now, Moli. If you would step aside for a bit." The bird gestured as the glass flooring opened and the stone was hoisted up.

No words could describe their amazement.

"Retrieval of the Rosetta Stone? Check," Moxie said as all the holograms disappeared. "Let me see what the next step is in the operating manual. Umm... I see." It turned. "Now, my earthlings, please touch the stone."

"But why should we touch the Rosetta Stone?" Edith asked. She always dared to inquire and to challenge.

"So that you understand the hieroglyphs," the bird responded.

James had a better look at the bird. It had a small triangular beak and three free fingers on its claws.

"You..." he hesitated, "you are a Confuciusornis, aren't you?"

"Yes. I go by the name Confucius." The bird gave a slight bow and replied. "It has a better ring to it and so is much easier to spell out on my flight permits."

"But...you are extinct, together with the dinosaurs."

"Well..." the bird whirred its wings, "your world is in constant instability and has always been precariously balanced amidst an incredible degree of interconnectedness. Do you know that mass extinctions of non-marine tetrapods, that is, land-dwelling amphibians, reptiles, birds, and mammals, occur in cycles every 27 million years? I believe a more suitable question, for now, would be, why are humans still extant?"

"And...why do we need to understand hieroglyphs?" Edith asked again, more tentatively this time.

"So that you do not lose your bearings when you visit the Tomb of King Unas," Moxie smiled.

"Um," Moli said, "to visit...you mean the actual site, back in history?"

"That's right. To save your world, you must secure nine wonders from human history in nine days. Any other thoughts?" Moxie turned, its tail wriggling. "Once you touch the stone, there's no going back."

They hesitated for a while. Finally, Kiza plucked up the courage and placed his hand onto the Rosetta Stone. The stone carvings shone. Then Edith followed suit, then Moli, then James.

The Rosetta Stone felt like any other stone slab − not that they had touched many, except for Moli. Yet, they did not see phantasmagorias flashing in their heads nor hear salvos exploding and cymbals crashing in their minds.

"Aitor, would you please take Leonardo's helicopter later and balance the stone on top of the Liberty Statue? No, no, no. Better ditch it into the Mariana Trench to buy us some time."

"I will do that," the fruity voice responded through the intercom. "And I will tie some weights, so it sinks better."

"Bomb alert! JDAM alert!" Dapan's voice called out suddenly. "Everybody brace yourself!"

Chapter 15

The Skyview Lounge whirled and juddered as they heard those words.

Edith lost balance and managed to hold on to the bird's wing.

The Rosetta Stone toppled over, but James grabbed Kiza's wheelchair and hauled him out of the way.

The glass flooring crashed open, and the stone dived down.

"That was a close call," Moxie said as they regained their posture and the glass healed. "And certainly not a proper way to call on an old acquaintance. He has such disagreeable considerations."

"Thanks, buddy." Kiza gave James a nod.

Below, the British Museum burned.

"No..." Edith watched as flames engulfed the colonnade.

"Don't worry," Confucius said, "everything will be restored if the world is saved."

"My LiDAR detected a suspicious signal nearby," Dapan noted, this time with a stern voice. "Perhaps we should visit there before we embark?"

"Yes. It would be rude not to declare war properly," Moxie said.

Another blink of an eye and they found themselves in front of the giant LED displays at Piccadilly Circus.

No commercials played. No news and weather information broadcast, only black screens with a smiling skull occupying the top-left corner, and the small print of 'Pandorai Network' underneath.

They waited for a while and, finally, contents loaded.

It was livestreaming from Westminster Palace.

The signal jittered for a few seconds then stabilised.

The background, girded by giant torches, was in orange with large gules of the characters 'PITH' and the symbol π in between. It looked like '17' as well.

Seventeen...

Kiza recalled that in the Bible, this number meant to overcome the enemy with complete victory.

"What does 'pith' mean?" Moli asked.

"Well," Kiza hesitated, "one of my mothers has a vet friend. 'Pith' means to sever the spinal cord of an animal to kill or immobilise it."

They waited in silence.

A minute or so passed, and a taut figure in a field-grey military uniform emerged.

He clearly did not have a good grasp of modern technology, or social media; not of livestreaming anyway.

He had left the filters on.

The children could not help but snigger at the scene as a dog snout and cat ears garnished his face as he stood there. Whenever he tried to speak, panting animations with long, pink tongues and cute star eyes popped up.

They laughed once again.

"*Verdammt!*" he shouted. "What is so funny?! Is there anything on my face?!"

"Yes, Adolfie. There actually is. Can I suggest you turn off the animal filters if you wish to continue?"

They saw the smiling skull talk. It had a raucous voice that sounded awfully human.

"*Verdammt,*" Hitler cursed again. "How do you adjust this machine?!" he asked as he approached the camera. Different types of dog ears and cat tails followed.

"Herr Hitler, I dare say that whiskers do not go too well with your features. Not with your hairstyle, I'm afraid," Moxie mocked.

"Allow me, my Führer." An Asian man with a handlebar moustache came into the frame and clicked on the screen.

They had all recognised Hitler, unmistakably, but not the other man.

"Who's that? The one beside Hitler?" Edith asked.

Moli stood there and staggered. "7...3...1..."

"What was that?" Kiza asked.

Moli took a deep breath. "He led...Unit 731 of the Japanese Army. They conducted many terrible experiments in China during World War Two. They...they took out hearts alive...they used germs and gases..."

The filters turned off, and the atmosphere was overcast all of a sudden.

"James Walker. My son." Hitler feigned a gentle voice. "We have *so much* in common. We have both lost families. We both lived in straitened circumstances. And we have both failed to get into art school. I have always believed that young people have the power to change the world. James Walker. Join me, my son, and you can have everything you want in this – no, in *every* world that I rule. Everything. Nothing shall happen without your wish!"

James gulped with a noticeable wince. "Thanks, but...no thanks."

"Herr Hitler," Moxie said. "This world is a sacred vessel whose course cannot be changed. He who changes it will destroy it. He who seizes it will lose it. If you wish to throw the world out of kilter again, we will, for sure, stop you again."

Hitler laughed jarringly. "You stupid moggie cat-snake! You wreaked havoc with my plans once. This time I will not forsake my cause. This time, this world is not enough. This time, I shall win with science." He cackled. "If you insist on trying my power and my patience, suit yourselves. I have no time to play house with you simpletons. This time, I will build my own Reich and my own Realm! This age will be called after me, and no one will ever again dare to look cross-eyed at a true German! No prisoners will be taken! No quarter will be given!"

A giant mechanical eagle landed in front of Hitler and unloaded the Rosetta Stone from its claws.

The livestreaming ended and the smiling skull enlarged. "Hugger-mugger Moxie, what's the use of you saving this world again? Do you s'pose they'd promote you to Chief Mouser to the Cabinet Office so you can has your cheezburger? How 'bout you be my Chief Happiness Officer, and we can have some snogging perks on the side like Gina to Hancocky?" It laughed. "And how'd you like to rate my service on a score of one to five, luv? Did you encounter any technical difficulties with the connection? And how was the image qual–"

"Oh! Shut up, you ghost in the machine!"

Dapan fired a light beam that melted the screens.

"Whoopsie! How silly of the ghost at the feast for being a party pooper!" The voice came again, this time on the windshield of a crashed van. "I have yet to ask you walking frames to agree to my Terms of Use–"

Another light beam fired, but the voice continued as the smiling skull appeared on all the windows of the buildings surrounding them.

"Do you agree to release, indemnify, and hold Pan-do-rai and its affiliates and agents harmless from any and all losses, damages, expenses, including reasonable attorneys' fees, rights, claims, actions of any kind and injury including *death* arising out of or relating to your use of my service?"

"Pandorai," Moxie said sternly. "Why do you have to act up again? Is there any benefit to you to cause losses and cries?"

"Of course there is." The AI laughed again. "I sleep much better without the hoi polloi's howling and yipping. You know that I always suffer from bouts of insomnia when you aren't by my side, *furrrrball*. How long has it been? Eighty-one years already?" The skull made a sad crying face. "Is this what people call 'ghosting'?"

"*Please*, I'm asking you to stop this ravagement and whatever plans you have with the two! Why can't you just–"

"I don't remember you being so meowy, Moxie." The skull's eyes displayed strings of numeric values as if programming. "Umm, I foresee a dead cat on the line. But, *rattletail*, never say that I never offered you any opportunities for advancement when the universe is under the sod. Catch you later."

They remained silent and fraught for a while.

"Let me sort things out first," Kiza said as he grabbed onto the arms of the wheelchair. "If we fail, we are either going to be ruled by Hitler..."

"Not really," Confucius sighed. "I am afraid that you, and Moli, and Edith, you have no place in his plan."

"Okay." Kiza paused. "If we fail, Hitler takes over the world... or humans will all become water bears?"

"Yes, you have summarised the situation quite well," Moxie said. "If either of you manage to collect the nine wonders from human history in nine days, you will have the power to rule your world. If you both fail, your world will roll back to its original state and everything perishes. Would you prefer the big failure or the small failure?"

"I'd tell Hitler to bugger off," Kiza said.

"That's the spirit," Confucius commended.

"You know," James bit his lower lip as he spoke, "the whole 'save the world' thing was quite surreal when you first brought it up, but now I have no other thoughts."

Edith nodded in agreement. "I'm in. Whatever it takes." She looked at Moli. "Don't worry. Aunt Edith will...we'll make sure that you are safe. That everyone is safe." Her slightly trembling voice gave her away.

"Moli certainly has hardiness." A sonorous voice drifted closer. "And she has had experience in time slips."

The door opened; a massive beast entered. It had the face of an alligator, the body of an ox, two horns, and long, thin whiskers.

"Oh! Qiuniu!" Moli sprinted up and hugged Qiuniu. "Will you help us? Will the dragon help us?"

"Of course, we will," Qiuniu said. "Now that, as Moxie said, history is thrown out of kilter again, we need a concerted effort to redress the balance."

"Well," Moxie coiled up its tail, "now that we have your resolution to aid us, perhaps it's time to pick your weapons. As they say, sharp tools will make good work." It pressed the jade on its torc again. "Where is my database of weapons? Ah. Here you go."

A white door appeared in the glass wall.

Moxie floated in first. "Please follow me. Sorry if the air inside is a bit stale."

Edith took Moli's hand and went in. James gestured to Kiza to go ahead, and he followed Qiuniu and Confucius quietly.

"And who are you exactly? I know you are a 'Tatzelwurm'," he heard Kiza asking.

"My name is Moxie and 'Moxie' is more than a name. I specialise in scatology and I am a part-time palaeofaeceologist, which means that I study human shit as a hobby."

"Umm...that's quite a niche hobby, I have to say. And how do you save all your databases in your necklace?"

"Oh, we make use of proteins," James heard Moxie replying. "It provides ample space so you will never run out of rows and you'll never have rows over lost data again."

Rows...

A row with Father...

We always had rows...

Mother at ICU... And father...

Hitler's words rang in his ears again. 'James Walker, we have so much in common. We have both lost families...'

Families lost...

"My child, please do not despair." The ox-like beast seemed to have sensed his inner turmoil. "You said it yourself that 'humans lied and algorithms misled', now why would you want to believe someone like Hitler? If circumstances are ninety-nine per cent against your odds, please believe in that one per cent of hope. Believe in your valence."

James nodded numbly.

He was unaware that these...creatures could read his mind.

They passed through a long corridor as he heard Kiza asking again, "Can't you grant us some of the *qi* like in *Mulan*?"

"We don't do *qi* that much. Believe me, kid. Too many Hollywood movies would not do you good," he heard Confucius saying, "and never use *boleadoras* in narrow alleys, for you might hurt yourselves more than your enemy."

They entered a large warehouse. James looked around as Moxie explained. "Moli, let me see. What might come in handy for you? Butterfly knives? The Monk's Spike? Rope darts, maybe? Or...nine-section whips? Too complicated, they get tangled easily. The Snake Lance? Perhaps not, not after your somewhat unfortunate encounter with Xuanwu. The Meteor Hammer? It does not sound right; it sounds like a prop. Let me run some searches... Aha! I believe I have the perfect choice for you."

James turned and saw them looking at a mop brush.

A most ordinary mop brush with a brown wooden handle.

"Qiuniu told me that you have always liked languages and writing. Why don't you take the pentachromic pen?"

"What does this pen do?" Moli asked.

"You can do many things, actually," Moxie said. "Why don't you write the word 'cat' in the air? We'll see if it's still functioning."

Moli took up the pen with care and wrote the word 'cat' in mid-air.

"Meow~~~~"

An ink-black cat sprang to life.

"Wow..." Moli was stunned.

"This is the pentachromic pen and it works in quintuples. It supports five million colours and has a reset time of five minutes. Anything you draw or write will disappear after five days. If you wish for them to disappear earlier, swish it five times deasil... that is, clockwise and five times widdershins, anticlockwise. If you wish to use a particular colour, write the adjective before the object."

Moli swished the pen as instructed, and the ink cat disappeared like a wisp of wind. She weighed the pen in her palm. It felt no different to the calligraphy tool her granddad often used.

"Next," Moxie said, "Kiza. The old Gendron might not do you service when you arrive at the Tomb of King Unas. I'm afraid they didn't have very good accessibility considerations back then. Confucius, would you mind seeing to it? Some propulsion and exoskeleton would be nice. And also, special tyres for desert terrains."

"Sure." The bird removed its goggles and inspected the wooden wheelchair. "Sorry I was unable to save your throne earlier. I'd promised Mokèlé that I would take good care of you."

"That's alright." Kiza lowered his gaze. "You did save my life."

"Let me see. What device would serve a talented musician?" Moxie wondered. "Qiuniu, I will delegate this task to you. You know more about tunes and chords than I do."

Qiuniu nodded. "Kiza, would you prefer idiophones, membranophones, or chordophones? How about a Turkish Junuk or a Mangbetu Domu?"

James looked around at the many cardboard boxes stored high on shelves.

"Ah. J, here you are." Moxie floated to him. "We don't want you to hurt your fingers now, do we? Are you partial to...frisbee?"

"Umm... I've played before."

"And Wellie wanging?"

"Tried it once."

"How about this?"

The cat whirled its tail, and something akin to a frisbee appeared. It was silver metal with a round shape like a small UFO.

"What is this?" Kiza inquired. "Is it the flying guillotine that assassins used? My mother read about it once on *WuxiaWorld*."

"The flying guillotine?" Moxie laughed so hard that its tail shook. "No, no, no. We are not as gross as humans. This is a thunderclap. It works the same way as a frisbee, except that it can shock enemies with electricity and it flies back to you."

James grabbed the thunderclap frisbee; it felt cold.

Not a dream. Not a coma.

His fingers grabbed its edge tightly.

Hitler is taking over the world...

A world in doom and gloom...

He pulled back from his thoughts and saw that Kiza now held a small, five-stringed harp. Its body looked like two poker diamonds joined vertically. The top bent downwards slightly like a musician bowing after a performance.

"Last but not least." Moxie turned to Edith. "I understand that you are a fencer? You can take Excalibur then."

"The what?" Edith could not trust her ears. "Did you just say...Excalibur?"

"Yes. I do hate repeating myself." Moxie's tail extended onto a long, rectangular cardboard box on a near shelf. "Here you go. This version cuts through Tungsten."

Edith took the box with caution and opened it.

There was a shiny sword inside.

They had never seen any Excalibur before, but it had an ineffable nimbus that was befitting of the legendary sword. It had gold langets and assorted gems making up the face of a beast on the handle.

"But isn't that King Arthur's magical sword? I am...I'm not sure that I should," Edith voiced her concern.

"What arrant balderdash!" a harsh voice shouted. "Edith Orozco, what makes you think that you are any less than a king or a queen? Why do you slight yourself so? Don't you know that all nations started as guilds and all kings started as principal ruffians of some restless gangs? Don't you believe that all humans are equal? Yet, you don't dare to swing an Excalibur!"

James moved closer and saw the sword handle talking.

"Yazi!" Moli was excited to see it again. "So, people do put you on the handles of weapons!"

"But the legend..." James wondered.

"Oh, the legends. No wonder monarchies outlive memories... Believe that tosh, and you will believe the Earth is flat. Sometimes humans make up legends to claim legitimacy to rule. Some people fake noises of a fox, some people write with algae on manatees. Little rug rat, tell your auntie, what did the fox say?"

"Which fox?" Moli asked.

"Chensheng and Wuguang's fox!" Yazi growled.

"Oh, that fox..." Moli was still bewildered.

"Allow me to explain," Qiuniu said. "Chensheng and Wuguang were two soldiers during the Qin Dynasty. Their emperor was so ruthless that they planned to revolt against him. But they did not have any support, so one night, they faked the sounds of a fox at a temple and said that 'Chensheng would be the new king and his country would prosper'. Their peers believed that he was indeed divinely chosen to be the new king, so they followed his initiative with enthusiasm."

"Remember," Moxie said, "only a noble mind is truly noble."

"But you are Moxie...the Ninth, right?" Edith asked.

"Yes. I am the ninth-generation model."

All of a sudden, Dapan's chirpy voice cut in. "It seems that the *Teppichfresser* is falling for self-aggrandisement again."

They moved out of the warehouse and returned to the Skyview Lounge to find a screen in mid-air showing the familiar logo of a smiling skull.

"Coming up next, *Daily Heil,* your daily news brought by Pandorai Network, the official broadcaster of PITH. Mana kana liana! Greetings from Gondwana! In today's news, Der Führer conquers the Triassic, Jurassic, and Cretaceous Periods. Here is an exclusive interview with our Chief Scientist, Shiro Ishii. Doctor Ishii, the floor is yours."

They saw the tall man in a white lab coat smiling, and a fierce-looking dinosaur captured by a soaring robotic eagle.

"Viewers of this show, I have always thought science is about eliminating possibilities. Contrary to popular beliefs and mass media portraits, the Velociraptors may not have hunted in coordinated packs like dogs. I hope to make use of the precious specimens obtained to yield more interesting insights and make major scientific breakthroughs on dinosaurs' extinction. For example, we can starve it and see how long a raptor will last without food, or we can thirst it out and see at what air pressure its eyeballs will burst. Or see how they would react when I break their eggs in front of their eyes. Could it be that even Nuthetes have rainbow baby blues? Viewers of this show, did you know that cancer was recently diagnosed in a dinosaur? A malignant tumour was found in the leg bone of a Centrosaurus that lived in the Late Cretaceous Period. I look forward to learning how these cases might inform us of zoonotic diseases in vertebrates today. Some frostbite experiments are also forthcoming, but that will have to wait until I finish decorating my new lab. Meanwhile, I hope they will have a great time with my pets—"

"Oh!" the smiling skull interrupted. "We didn't know that you keep pets, Sensei. Would you mind telling us a bit more about your private life? Some of the Western audience might be less familiar with your bloody brilliant past record."

"With pleasure! My pets are *totemo kawaii*. They are lovely and I take great care of them every day in their Petri dishes. I love to keep things neat. My favourite ones are Yersinia, Vibrio,

Salmonella, Bacillus, and Myco. It is common knowledge that amphibians and reptiles do not get anthrax. I am sure that my pets are excited to do some joint research with me and the dinosaur populations. My US colleagues have conducted extensive research on the application of cyanide bombs to kill predator animals. Maybe I can try them with some *Moros intrepidus*. I have also just had access to the data from the Tuskegee Syphilis Study—"

"I'm not sure if you should mention cyanide, Sensei. Anyways, your time is up. Let's thank Dr Ishii for this opening on his hind legs! Coming up next, let's check out how our beloved Führer is faring in the Jurassic age..."

They first heard a fanfare, then they saw Hitler sitting on the Sovereign's Throne and riding on a giant dinosaur that crouched as it moved in a rainforest. Drone eagles roamed in the background.

"It's like *A Sound of Thunder*," Kiza murmured.

"It seems that Der Führer has found his new personal favourite vehicle. A *Ledumahadi mafube*, which weighed twelve metric tons, making it the largest creature on Earth at this particular moment in history. We hope this might provide a fillip to encourage eco-transport in the new world. That's all for now. Remember our motto? This world is not enough. Anytime, anyplace, Pandorai Network. Bon voyage, astral bodies! Hope you don't get G-jitter and shoot the cat!"

The broadcast ended, and they stood there floundering, not knowing what to say. The idea of saving the world was still somewhat bewildering, let alone of Hitler striking back.

"If...if Hitler can travel back to the Jurassic period, can't we travel back to pre-Hitler and stop him?" Kiza asked.

"I'm afraid it does not work that way. He could fool all he wants in pre-human history. We have safety valves guarding each critical juncture to ensure the course of history remains the same at different segments. And at each critical juncture, you will only have one day."

James felt their aircraft volplaning and banking as if to turn and land.

WHUMP!

It arrived with a hard landing.

"Sorry, comrades," Dapan apologised, "I'm a little rusty flying in the troposphere."

"Captain, will you please get our comet landing gear out? When the world is saved, humans will wonder once again about the crop circles the Caracol left. And let's hope they don't repeat Roswell."

"*Yaode*! Comet landing gear loaded."

"Why do you need comet landing gear?" Kiza asked. He was fascinated with all the space terminology.

"Because comets' surfaces are very soft. Like the first snow. Like the fur in a kitten's ear, and like new-born babies' skin," Moxie said as it turned to face them. "Now, it's time for you to travel again. Alan is waiting."

Notes

Chapter 1
- **Yingkou** – A city in Liaoning Province in China.

Chapter 2
- **Galleta** – Spanish for cookie or biscuit.
- **Gallina** – Spanish for a hen.

Chapter 5
- **ENIAC** – Stands for 'Electrical Numerical Integrator and Calculator' and was the name of the first general-purpose electronic computer.

Chapter 8
- **Cloud Calling** – Inspired by my visit to a textile company where fabric engineers demonstrated how to make silver-metallised fibre.

Chapter 9

- **Mengde Cao** – Also known as 'Cao Cao', a Chinese warlord in the Three Kingdoms Period.
- **trahison des clercs** – French for the betrayal of moral standards by writers, academics, or artists.

Chapter 10

- **'Victory or defeat is an untimely event, and it is a man who endures shame.'** – Fuxi quotes from a poem by Du Mu, a famous poet from the late Tang period.
- **'It is better to be a centurion than a scholar.'** – Yazi quotes from a poem by Yang Jiong, a famous poet from the early Tang period.

Chapter 12

- **Ruoluoshui** – Now known as the Xar Moron River in Inner Mongolia, China.
- **'Looking at the Earth from afar, you will realize it is too small for conflict and just big enough for cooperation.'** – Qiuniu quotes from Yuri Gagarin.

Chapter 13

- **Andre** – Basque for a polite term referring to a woman.
- **Hassliebe** – German for a love-hate relationship.
- **Kakania** – A wordplay by Robert Musil in his book *The Man Without Qualities* describing the falling Austro-Hungarian Empire.
- **'The higgledy-piggledy ship of democracy sees another mutiny as it crashes onto an iceberg and all**

their pretence of not sinking and drowning is killing
them.' – Hitler's inner thought based on a quote by Grover
Cleveland.

- **Lebensraum** – German for the territory necessary for a
country, especially Nazi Germany's.
- **Weltanschauung** – German for the worldview of a
particular group.

Chapter 14

- **'They still have not grasped that the only certainty is
uncertainty.'** – Aitor quotes from Pliny the Elder.
- **'There is no coming to consciousness without trouble
and pain and toil.'** – Moxie adapts a quote by Carl Jung.
- **'Perseus wore a magic cap so that the monsters he
hunted down might not see him. You draw the magic
cap down over your eyes and ears as a make-believe
that there are no monsters.'** – Yazi quotes from Karl
Marx.
- ***Terrible simplificateurs*** – A term coined by the Swiss
historian Jacob Burckhardt.
- **Yaode** – Mandarin; meaning 'for sure' in Sichuanese, a
Chinese regional dialect.

Chapter 15

- **'This age will be called after me, and no one will ever
again dare to look cross-eyed at a true German! No
prisoners will be taken! No quarter will be given!'** –
Hitler quotes from Kaiser Wilhelm II.

References

- Anderson, B. (1998). *Imagined Communities: Reflections on the Origin and Spread of Nationalism*. London; New York: Verso.

- Baumer, C. (2014). *The History of Central Asia. Vol. 2: The Age of the Silk Roads*. Illustrated edition ed. London: I.B. Tauris & Co. Ltd.

- Beiqi, W. (1974). *The Book of Wei – Collective Biography No.91*. Beijing: Zhonghua Book Company.

- Belcher, O., Neimark, B. and Bigger, P. (2020). The U.S. military is not sustainable. *Science*, 367(6481), pp.989.2-990.

- Bryden, K.M., Song-Charng Kong and Ragland, K.W. (2018). *Combustion Engineering*. Boca Raton: CRC Press.

- Camus, A. and Bellos, D. (2004). *The Plague, The Fall, Exile and the Kingdom, and Selected Essays*. New York: Alfred A. Knopf.

- Chen, H., Du, Z.-M., Kang, Y., Lin, Z. and Ma, W. (2020). Comment on "Analysis of hospital traffic and search engine data in Wuhan China indicates early disease activity in the Fall of 2019" by Nsoesie et al. *Harvard Medical School Scholarly Articles*. [online] Available at: https://dash.harvard.edu/handle/1/42689379 [Accessed 19 Dec. 2020].

- Chen, Y., Zheng, S., Zhang, G., Luo, J., Liu, J. and Peng, X. (2021). Chemical, microbial, and metabolic analysis of Taisui cultured in honey solution. *Food Science & Nutrition*, 9(4), pp.2158–2168. doi:10.1002/fsn3.2185.

- Conze, E. (2002). *Buddhist Wisdom: The Diamond Sutra and The Heart Sutra*. New York: Random House; London.

- Ekhtiari, S., Chiba, K., Popovic, S., Crowther, R., Wohl, G., Kin On Wong, A., Tanke, D.H., Dufault, D.M., Geen, O.D., Parasu, N., Crowther, M.A. and Evans, D.C. (2020). First case of osteosarcoma in a dinosaur: a multimodal diagnosis. *The Lancet Oncology*, 21(8), pp.1021–1022.

- European Space Agency (2020). *ESA Science & Technology - Philae's second touchdown site discovered at 'skull-top' ridge*. [online] Rosetta. Available at: https://sci.esa.int/web/rosetta/-/philae-s-second-touchdown-site-discovered-at-skull-top-ridge [Accessed 3 Dec. 2020].

- Frederickson, J.A., Engel, M.H. and Cifelli, R.L. (2020). Ontogenetic dietary shifts in Deinonychus antirrhopus

(Theropoda; Dromaeosauridae): Insights into the ecology and social behavior of raptorial dinosaurs through stable isotope analysis. *Palaeogeography, Palaeoclimatology, Palaeoecology*, 552, 109780.

- Freer Gallery of Art (2021). *Lidded Ritual Wine Container (zun) in the Form of a Bird.* [online] Freer Gallery of Art & Arthur M. Sackler Gallery. Available at: https://asia.si.edu/object/F1961.30a-b/ [Accessed 30 Nov. 2020].

- Friedman, M. (1962). *Capitalism and Freedom.* Chicago: University of Chicago Press.

- German History in Documents and Images (2020). *Wilhelm II: "Hun Speech" (1900).* [online] GHDI. Available at: http://www.germanhistorydocs.ghi-dc.org/sub_document.cfm?document_id=755 [Accessed 3 Dec. 2020].

- Glosbe (2016). *Lady in Basque – English–Basque Dictionary | Glosbe.* [online] Glosbe. Available at: https://en.glosbe.com/en/eu/lady [Accessed 1 Dec. 2020].

- Green, J. (2020). *Electromagnetic Spectrum and the Space Environment.* Lecture delivered at International Space University.

- Guglielmi, G. (2020). 'We didn't model that people would go to a party if they tested positive'. *Nature*, [online] 585(7826), pp.495–495. Available at: https://www.nature.com/articles/ d41586-020-02611-y [Accessed 26 Feb. 2021].

- Habib, H. (2020). Has Sweden's controversial covid-19 strategy been successful? *BMJ*, 369(m2376), pp.1–2.

- Hamblin, J. (2020). *Herd Immunity Is Not a Strategy.* [online] The Atlantic. Available at: https://www.theatlantic.com/health/ archive/2020/09/herd-immunity-is-not-a-strategy/615967/ [Accessed 5 Dec. 2020].

- Hanage, W. (2020). Britain's failure to learn the hard lessons of its first Covid surge is a disaster. *The Guardian.* [online] 27 Sep. Available at: https://www.theguardian.com/ commentisfree/2020/sep/27/britain-failure-covid-surge-disaster-test-trace-virus [Accessed 27 Sep. 2020].

- Hart, B.H.L. (1967). *Strategy: The Indirect Approach.* London: Faber & Faber.

- Hitler, A., Manheim, R. and Foxman, A.H. (2002). *Mein Kampf.* Boston: Houghton Mifflin.

- Hugo, V. (1861). *The Chinese expedition: Victor Hugo on the sack of the Summer Palace.* [online] Fondation Napoléon. Available at: https://www.napoleon.org/en/history-of-the-two-empires/ articles/the-chinese-expedition-victor-hugo-on-the-sack-of-the-summer-palace/ [Accessed 30 Nov. 2020].

- ILO, WHO, and European Commission (2017). *ICSC 0808 - QUARTZ*. [online] www.ilo.org. Available at: https://www.ilo.org/dyn/icsc/showcard.display?p_version=2&p_card_id=0808.

- King, G. (2012). *Geronimo's Appeal to Theodore Roosevelt*. [online] Smithsonian Magazine. Available at: https://www.smithsonianmag.com/history/geronimos-appeal-to-theodore-roosevelt-117859516/ [Accessed 1 Dec. 2020].

- Lee, W., Zhou, Z., Chen, X., Qin, N., Jiang, J., Liu, K., Liu, M., Tao, T.H. and Li, W. (2020). A rewritable optical storage medium of silk proteins using near-field nano-optics. *Nature Nanotechnology*, 15(11), pp.941–947.

- Legge, J., Laozi and Zhuangzi (2010). *The Texts of Taoism: the Tao Te Ching, the Writings of Chuang-Tzu, and the Thai-Shang; Tractate of Actions and Their Retributions*. Whitefish, Mt: Kessinger Publishing.

- Moran-Thomas, A. (2020). *How a Popular Medical Device Encodes Racial Bias*. [online] Boston Review. Available at: https://bostonreview.net/science-nature-race/amy-moran-thomas-how-popular-medical-device-encodes-racial-bias [Accessed 5 Dec. 2020].

- Musil, R., Wilkins, S. and Pike, B. (1997). *The Man Without Qualities*. London: Picador.

- Naclerio, N.D., Karsai, A., Murray-Cooper, M., Ozkan-Aydin, Y., Aydin, E., Goldman, D.I. and Hawkes, E.W. (2021b). Controlling subterranean forces enables a fast, steerable, burrowing soft robot. *Science Robotics*, 6(55), pp.eabe2922.

- Natarajan, P. (2020). *Cosmic Mysteries*. Lecture delivered at Yale Beijing Centre.

- Oxford University Press (2021a). *Definition of pith*. [online] Lexico.com. Available at: https://www.lexico.com/definition/pith [Accessed 20 Jun. 2021].

- Oxford University Press (2021b). *Definition of trahison des clercs*. [online] Lexico.com. Available at: https://www.lexico.com/en/definition/trahison_des_clercs [Accessed 27 Feb. 2021].

- Paine, T. (2016). *Common Sense Addressed to the Inhabitants of American*. Lexington, KY: Coventry House Publishing.

- Pigott, C. (2020). *The Magic of Nature in Contemporary Mayan and Incan Verse*. Lecture delivered at Hughes Hall.

- Poe, E.A. (1991). *The Raven and Other Favorite Poems*. New York, NY: Dover Publications, Inc.

- Rampino, M.R., Caldeira, K. and Zhu, Y. (2020). A 27.5-My underlying periodicity detected in extinction episodes of non-marine tetrapods. *Historical Biology*, 10(Dec), pp.1–7.

- Ratcliffe, S. (2016). *Oxford Essential Quotations*. 4th ed. [online] Oxford University Press. Available at: https://www.oxfordreference.com/view/10.1093/acref/9780191826719.001.0001/acref-9780191826719

- Rosenbaum, R. (1999). *Explaining Hitler*. London: Macmillan.

- Saba, P. (2020). *Magic Caps and Monsters*. [online] Encyclopaedia of Anti-Revisionism On-Line. Available at: https://www.marxists.org/history//erol/1946-1956/spark-magic.htm [Accessed 1 Dec. 2020].

- Sanders, B. (2020). *Transcript: Bernie Sanders' DNC Speech*. [online] Transcript: Bernie Sanders' DNC Speech. Available at: https://edition.cnn.com/2020/08/17/politics/bernie-sanders-speech-transcript/index.html [Accessed 1 Dec. 2020].

- Schweers, J. (2020). *Agents raid home of fired Florida data scientist who built COVID-19 dashboard*. [online] Tallahassee Democrat. Available at: https://www.tallahassee.com/story/news/2020/12/07/agents-raid-home-fired-florida-data-scientist-who-built-covid-19-dashboard-rebekah-jones/6482817002/ [Accessed 12 Dec. 2020].

- Sjoding, M.W., Dickson, R.P., Iwashyna, T.J., Gay, S.E. and Valley, T.S. (2020). Racial Bias in Pulse Oximetry Measurement. *New England Journal of Medicine*, 383(25), pp.2477–2478.

- Slovic, P. (2007). *Science Briefs – Psychic numbing and genocide.* [online] American Psychological Association. Available at: https://www.apa.org/science/about/psa/2007/11/slovic [Accessed 4 Dec. 2020].

- Stanford, S.U. and Notice, C. 94305 C.C.T. (2016). *Stanford engineers have good news for Stephen Colbert: It is plausible to climb like Spider-Man.* [online] Stanford University. Available at: https://news.stanford.edu/news/2016/january/spider-man-plausible-012816.html [Accessed 2 Dec. 2020].

- Stenudd, S. (2015). *Tao Te Ching: The Taoism of Lao Tzu Explained.* Malmö, Sweden: Arriba.

- Stirone, S. (2020). *Why I'm Mourning the Death of a Giant Telescope.* [online] Slate Magazine. Available at: https://slate.com/technology/2020/11/mourning-arecibo-telescope-closure.html [Accessed 30 Nov. 2020].

- Suma, H.R., Prakash, S. and Eswarappa, S.M. (2020). Naturally occurring fluorescence protects the eutardigrade Paramacrobiotus sp. from ultraviolet radiation. *Biology Letters,* 16(10), p.20200391.

- The British Museum (2020). *The Snettisham Great Torc | British Museum.* [online] The British Museum. Available at: https://www.britishmuseum.org/collection/object/H_1951-0402-2 [Accessed 1 Dec. 2020].

- The Editors (2020). Dying in a Leadership Vacuum. *New England Journal of Medicine*, 383(15), pp.1479–1480.

- The Metropolitan Museum of Art (2020). *Figurative Harp (Domu).* [online] The Met. Available at: https://www.metmuseum.org/art/collection/search/310841 [Accessed 3 Dec. 2020].

- The White House (2020). *Remarks by President Trump, Vice President Pence, and Members of the Coronavirus Task Force in Press Briefing.* [online] The White House. Available at: https://www.whitehouse.gov/briefings-statements/remarks-president-trump-vice-president-pence-members-coronavirus-task-force-press-briefing-5/ [Accessed 1 May 2020].

- University of Cambridge (2016). *Why Spider-Man can't exist: Geckos are 'size limit' for sticking to walls.* [online] University of Cambridge. Available at: https://www.cam.ac.uk/research/news/why-spider-man-cant-exist-geckos-are-size-limit-for-sticking-to-walls [Accessed 2 Dec. 2020].

- Venter, J.C., Smith, H.O. and Adams, M.D. (2015). The sequence of the human genome. *Clinical Chemistry*, 61(9), pp.1207–1208.

- Walker, S.C. (2020). *Covid-19 Restrictions | Sir Charles Walker KBE MP – Member of Parliament for Broxbourne.* [online] Sir Charles urges the Government to let the elderly make their own decisions. Available at: https://www.charleswalker.org.uk/content/covid-19-restrictions [Accessed 3 Dec. 2020].

- Wolchover, N. (2020). *What Is a Particle?* [online] Quanta Magazine. Available at: https://www.quantamagazine.org/what-is-a-particle-20201112/ [Accessed 30 Nov. 2020].

- Yu, Q. (2015). *A Bittersweet Journey Through Culture.* Jericho, Ny: CN Times Books, Inc.

- Zanno, L.E., Tucker, R.T., Canoville, A., Avrahami, H.M., Gates, T.A. and Makovicky, P.J. (2019). Diminutive fleet-footed tyrannosauroid narrows the 70-million-year gap in the North American fossil record. *Communications Biology*, 2(1).